"What are you doing here?"

Esther suddenly felt nervous and climbed down from the buggy to speak to Jacob. "I can't stay. I won't keep you from your work. I've just come to ask you for a favor."

Jacob looked at her quizzically.

"*Mamm*'s trying to match me with Amos Troyer," she began.

"Amos?" Jacob interrupted her. "That good-looking *mann*?"

Esther nodded. "*Jah.*"

Jacob frowned. "So, you think he's good-looking?"

"Well, *jah*, but that's not the point." Esther wondered why Jacob was looking a little annoyed.

Jacob let go of the horse's bridle and crossed his arms over his chest. "Have you come to tell me that you're dating Amos Troyer?"

"*Nee*, Jacob. I came to tell you that my *mudder* wants me to date Amos, but I don't want to." Jacob was sure acting weird. "Anyway," she continued, "*Mamm* has her heart set on me dating Amos, so...would you mind if we pretended that we were dating?"

Ruth Hartzler is an internationally bestselling and award-winning author of clean and sweet romance, mystery and suspense, including Amish romance, Christian romance and Christian cozy mysteries. Ruth is the recipient of several All-Star Awards (author and book).

THE WAY FORWARD

Ruth Hartzler

If you purchased this book without a cover you should be aware that this book is stolen property. It was reported as "unsold and destroyed" to the publisher, and neither the author nor the publisher has received any payment for this "stripped book."

ISBN-13: 978-1-335-49970-7

Recycling programs for this product may not exist in your area.

The Way Forward

First published in 2015 by Ruth Hartzler.
This edition published in 2019.

Copyright © 2015 by Ruth Hartzler

Scripture quotations are from The Holy Bible, English Standard Version ® (ESV ®), copyright © 2001 by Crossway, a publishing ministry of Good News Publishers. Used by permission. All rights reserved.

All rights reserved. Except for use in any review, the reproduction or utilization of this work in whole or in part in any form by any electronic, mechanical or other means, now known or hereafter invented, including xerography, photocopying and recording, or in any information storage or retrieval system, is forbidden without the written permission of the publisher, Harlequin Enterprises Limited, 22 Adelaide St. West, 40th Floor, Toronto, Ontario M5H 4E3, Canada.

This is a work of fiction. Names, characters, places and incidents are either the product of the author's imagination or are used fictitiously, and any resemblance to actual persons, living or dead, business establishments, events or locales is entirely coincidental.

This edition published by arrangement with Harlequin Books S.A.

For questions and comments about the quality of this book, please contact us at CustomerService@Harlequin.com.

® and TM are trademarks of Harlequin Enterprises Limited or its corporate affiliates. Trademarks indicated with ® are registered in the United States Patent and Trademark Office, the Canadian Intellectual Property Office and in other countries.

Printed in U.S.A.

THE WAY FORWARD

Chapter One

Esther tucked a loose curl under her prayer *kapp*, turning her gaze onto the pleasant summer afternoon. Laughing children sat among the bluebells, the faint breeze ruffling their dark and simple clothes. The older boys worked with their fathers in the great barns strung along the blue horizon, while the older girls worked in the gardens with their kind and honest mothers. The sight sent a shiver along Esther's spine. Since the accident, when a car had driven into their *familye* buggy, she had not been able to help her mother as much as she had wished.

"Lost in thought?" Esther jumped as Jacob Hostetler settled on the warm grass next to her, placing a string of wheat between his lips and stretching out his golden limbs. "Where do you go, Esther, when your mind drifts, I wonder?"

"I was thinking of my *familye*," Esther replied, honestly.

"Ah." Jacob took the wheat from his mouth. His

smile was crooked, and Esther had always found it charming. "You mean, you were thinking about *our familye*?"

That was true. Esther's older *schweschder*, Hannah, had married Jacob's older *bruder*, Noah, only recently. Hannah had beamed that morning, as she slipped on her blue linen dress, before she had married her best friend. After the ceremony, everyone enjoyed a feast of roast chicken, mashed potatoes and creamed celery and coleslaw, lemonade and ice cream and cherry pie. The celebration, the Singing, and the square dancing, had gone on well into the night.

"That's true. Anyway, what are you doing, Jacob? I thought you'd be helping your *vadder* and *bruders* with the farming at this time of the afternoon?"

"*Jah*, they do need my help, but *Mamm* sent me to check on you and your *schweschders*. How is everyone? I must say, it's nice to see you up and about again, Esther. I missed my little friend."

"I'm well, *denki*. I can even start to help with all the chores soon." The thought made Esther very happy indeed. "It'll be good to help *Mamm* around the *haus* and garden, since Martha and Rebecca aren't ready to do a lot of the chores. We're all looking forward to the day we can get back into our routine."

Esther gazed searchingly at the lake, where the early summer breeze played among the weeds, and ducks struck across the glimmering surface. She remembered the winter morning when Noah Hostetler had struck her *familye* buggy with his borrowed, ancient car when on his *rumspringa*. The accident was not his fault, given that the road was icy and the morning full of mist, and Hannah, who was the least injured of the four Miller *schweschders*, had not only finally forgiven him, but had married him. Still, Noah's *familye* had felt quite protective over the Miller *schweschders* since then. Perhaps that was why Jacob's *mudder* had sent him to check up on her, Martha and Rebecca.

"I'm glad to hear it," drawled Jacob.

Esther turned her attention back to Jacob. "How are your two younger *bruders*, Moses and Elijah?"

Jacob laughed. "We're as loud as ever. *Mamm's* always talking about the noise. She likes that about us, though I do think she's glad to have a *dochder* in the *familye* now. Did you ever think Noah and Hannah would marry?"

"In a way," Esther replied, "I suppose I always did."

"*Jah*." Jacob lay down on his back, letting the warm sunlight press into his handsome face. He truly was handsome, Esther thought, but then again all of the Hostetler brothers were. They were also compassionate and hardworking. All the girls in the community melted at the sight of them. Now that she thought about it, Jacob would probably be the next brother to marry. Esther wondered which of the lucky girls it would be.

Suddenly Jacob sat up, frowning. "What?" he said.

"I never said a thing," Esther said, defensively.

"I know you, Esther Miller." He ran a large hand through his sweep of golden hair. "You were thinking something about me, and I'm sure it's something I wouldn't approve of."

Esther pouted at him. "Was not!"

"Hmm," Jacob said, furrowing his brows. There was a cheeky twinkle in his eyes. "You're marrying me off!" he cried, all of a sudden. "Can't a *mann* sit by the lake with his oldest friend, without her plotting out his entire future? Go on, then. Who are you setting me up with in that romantic mind of yours, Esther?"

"I hadn't picked anyone specifically," she conceded. "I just thought you might be the next *bruder* to marry, seeing as Noah's happily married to my *schweschder*."

"I knew it." Jacob sighed. "At the very least, can you set me up with someone who's kind? Perhaps you could pick someone with a lot of siblings. I love all my *bruders*, so it would be nice to marry a girl who understands how important siblings are."

Esther bit her lip. "Who has a lot of siblings?" she wondered out loud. "Oh, I know! There's Sarah Hilty. She has three *bruders* and a *schweschder*. I can actually see you married to her. You'd make a very fine couple."

"Sarah Hilty's very nice," said Jacob, scrunching up his nose.

"But?"

"She must have more than just siblings. I also want a woman who's sweet, who thinks about her *familye*, and who would always see it in her heart to forgive those might have made a mistake."

"What about Jane Graber?"

"Jane!" Jacob sat up again with a startled expression on his face. "Why on earth would you think of Jane Graber?"

Esther grinned. "You seem a little too against Jane Graber. Do you have a secret crush on someone else, Jacob? Look, you're blushing now. I've never seen you blush before."

"*Nee, nee,*" said Jacob, scratching his chin. "It's just that I also want a girl who has a good imagination."

"But Jane's ideal then," Esther exclaimed, with a triumphant cry. She startled the ducks in the lake—they flapped their wings and vanished into the line of trees. "She's a very imaginative person."

Jacob sighed. "*Nee,*" he replied. Now he turned the full brilliance of his eyes onto Esther. "I wasn't thinking of Jane at all."

Chapter Two

The fluffy yellow ducklings followed their parents across the calm surface of the lake, with all the speed and determination of tired snails. Esther, Martha, and Rebecca sat on the bank, the water lapping pleasantly against their bare toes. It was good to shrug off the heavy woolen cloak worn in the cool winter months, Esther thought, as she threw some bread crumbs toward her new friend, a duck with only one leg. It felt nice to sit in the sunlight with two of her three *schweschders* and Mary, who had been sent by the bishop to help Mrs. Miller after the accident that had left all the Miller girls injured.

"But you did like him," Martha insisted. She and Rebecca had been teasing Esther about Jacob Hostetler for the past ten minutes, and Esther was trying her best to ignore their jokes.

"You had a crush on him for ages and ages," Rebecca chimed in, much to Martha's delight. "Handsome Jacob and his crooked smile. Martha and I thought you'd marry him without a thought."

Esther shook her head. No matter what she replied to her cheeky little sisters, neither would believe her protestations. She threw another crumb of bread to her aquatic friend. Like Esther, Rebecca and Martha were not yet quite well enough to return to their full chores, although they had all but recovered from their injuries received when Noah ran into their buggy. Their mother had given Esther half a loaf of bread and told her three youngest daughters to go and feed the ducks, happy to see them on their feet again after the accident. She had permitted Mary to go with them.

"You definitely did like him," Martha said to Esther.

"Look at the pretty green on that big duck," Esther murmured. "Don't you just love the purple shine on his feathers?"

"Liked who?" Martha said. "Who did you like, Esther? And did he like you back? I wish a boy would like me and I could like him back." Mary threw herself on the ground next to the Miller sisters. "Do you think I'll ever get married?"

"Of course you will get married," Esther said.

Mary sighed. "I hope I can stay here. You're all well now so I'm worried your mother will send me back home."

"You don't want to go home?" Esther asked her.

Mary plucked a piece of grass and twirled it around between her fingers. "*Nee*. I like it fine here."

"*Mamm* likes having you around and I'm sure you

can stay in the community even when I've fully recovered," Rebecca ventured.

Mary beamed. "Do you really think so?"

"Who do you have a crush on then, Esther?" Rebecca said, clearly growing a little annoyed now. She was the most persistent of the Miller sisters, and the youngest, and she was still learning how to be patient with the feelings of others.

"Okay, I used to like Jacob," Esther conceded.

"We knew it!" Rebecca swapped a smile with Martha. "I knew we'd get it out of you in the end. Imagine if you married Jacob, then you and Hannah would be very happy."

Esther shook her head. "I don't like him anymore. I was young and silly then, and we're only good friends. He's one of my best friends, now I come to think of it. But that's all, Rebecca."

Her little sisters exchanged glances once more. Rebecca opened her mouth to speak, but Martha threw a piece of bread at her. The two of them collapsed into helpless giggles, but then Martha's face turned serious. "Esther, I'm sure Jacob really likes you. Don't encourage him."

Esther chuckled. "Oh, Jacob doesn't like me like *that*! We're just friends. Anyway," she continued, ignoring Martha's raised eyebrows, "why all the questions? You can have him if you want, Martha."

"Who, me?" Martha was aghast. "I'm not going to date any Amish boy. I'm waiting until I go on *rumspringa*, then I might find myself a nice *Englisch* boy. Who knows!"

Esther's mouth fell open. "Martha, you can't!"

Martha squared her jaw. "Why not? I want my own chocolate business and I'll need a computer for that. Anyway, just because you and Hannah didn't want to go on *rumspringa*, doesn't mean I don't. I want to see what the *Englisch* world's like. I want to put on makeup and wear *Englisch* clothes, and drive a car, all of it. I want to play video games and watch television. I don't know why you're so against it."

Esther thought for a moment. There was a good reason the youth were allowed to go on *rumspringa*. Why, bishops and the whole communities approved of it, so who was she to make any comments? "No, you're right, Martha. Just because I didn't, doesn't mean you can't, of course. Just don't do anything reckless."

Martha simply giggled and threw more crumbs to the ducks, which were vying for every piece of bread. "Just as well you don't like Jacob Hostetler then," Martha said, "as you know how *Mamm* feels about the Hostetlers, ever since Noah ran the car into our buggy."

Esther stood up, somewhat stiffly, taking care not to hurt her back. "Nonsense, Martha. Hannah and Noah Hostetler are married now. *Mamm's* over all that these days." Even as she said the words, Esther knew they weren't quite true. She was sure her *mudder* still held some resentment toward the Hostetler *familye*. It was just as well that she did only see Jacob as a friend, as she was certain that her *mudder* would not permit another of her *dochders* to marry one of the Hostetler *bruders*.

Chapter Three

The second Esther laid eyes on the handsome Amos Troyer sitting on her porch, she knew her *mudder* was up to her old matchmaking tricks again. Of course, Esther had known Amos since childhood, but the Troyer and Miller *familyes* had never been overly close. Esther supposed her *mudder* was alarmed by the fact that her oldest *dochder* had already married a Hostetler boy, and there were three more eligible Hostetler boys remaining.

"Amos is here for dinner," Mrs. Miller announced.

Esther simply raised her eyebrows and nodded. "*Hiya*, Amos."

"*Hullo*, Esther."

While her *mudder* chatted to Amos, Esther took the opportunity to study Amos more closely. He was tall, with broad shoulders and blonde, almost wavy hair. His blue eyes contrasted attractively with his tanned face. *He's good-looking, that's for sure*, Esther thought, *but I don't get that feeling that some-*

one should get, despite what the ministers say. The ministers were always saying that feelings were less important than the qualities of humility, hard work, and piety in a prospective marriage partner.

Mrs. Miller waved a quart saucepan at Esther. "Esther, give your back a rest. You too, Rebecca. Martha and Mary can help me in the kitchen." Mrs. Miller, Martha, and Mary left for the kitchen, leaving Esther relieved that her *mudder* hadn't summoned Rebecca too, leaving Esther alone with Amos. That was the sort of thing she'd normally do.

Was it Esther's imagination, or did Amos look longingly in Martha's direction after she left? *Perhaps* Mamm *should put her matchmaking efforts toward Amos and Martha*, Esther thought.

Martha returned carrying a tray with glasses of lemonade, and set each glass of lemonade on the porch table. After everyone had thanked her, she said somewhat dramatically, "You're welcome. Sit and relax. You two had back injuries—I *only* had a broken arm and *two* broken legs." Martha disappeared through the door in a fit of indignation.

Esther caught her breath at Martha's rudeness, but Amos laughed out loud. "Your *schweschder* has spirit."

"*Jah*." Esther didn't know what else to say. Amos gave her a beaming smile and she smiled back politely. *Perhaps I was wrong about him liking Martha*, she thought. *He does seem to be smiling at me a bit too widely. What will I do? I don't want Amos to think he has any chance of courting me.*

The conversation flowed awkwardly, despite both Esther and Rebecca making an effort to include Amos in the conversation. Amos, Esther noted, seemed a little nervous. He kept rubbing the back of his neck and scratching at his chin.

Finally, Martha poked her head around the door to tell everyone to come inside for dinner. Esther inhaled deeply as she smelled the delicious odor of the Six Layer Dinner, one of her favorites, wafting through the door. She, her sisters, and Mary had peeled the potatoes and sliced the onions earlier, in preparation. There was nothing nicer than a meaty aroma mixed with onions, tomatoes and green peppers. Esther's mouth watered at the thought.

Just then, her *daed* came over from his woodworking workshop, and he and Amos exchanged greetings.

Esther saw Noah's buggy leave, and the big, black horse was going along at a good speed, his hooves making a rhythmic clip-clop. *Noah must be in a hurry to get home to Hannah*, she thought, amused. Noah and Hannah lived not far away, in a little *haus* that adjoined the Millers' property. Normally, they would spend their first few months as a married couple in the Millers' *haus*, but Hannah's broken leg had not healed as well as the *doktor* had liked. He had ordered Hannah to spend six weeks of complete rest prior to her marriage and had insisted that she must not walk up stairs for the best part of a year, possibly longer. The Hostetlers had then purchased a little *haus* for Noah and Hannah. The *haus* had been built by *Englischers* and was conveniently adjoining the

Millers' property. It was ideal, as it was all on one level and had no stairs, apart from two on the porch, and given the fact that Noah worked in Mr. Miller's woodworking business, he only had a short distance to drive the buggy to work each day.

The Miller *familye* and Amos sat down at the table, put their hands in their laps, and bowed their heads for the silent prayer. Mr. Miller was the first to speak to Amos. "So, how's the construction business going?"

Amos smiled. "*Gut, denki.*"

"So, what sort of construction do you do, Amos?" As soon as she spoke, Esther silently chastised herself. She didn't want to appear too interested in Amos. After all, she didn't want to give him the wrong idea.

Amos's fork halted half way to his mouth. "Gazebos, mainly. The *Englischers* love them. It's hard to keep up with demand."

"*Wunderbar*," Mrs. Miller exclaimed. "It is *gut* that your business is going so strongly, and you being such a young man. You will be a *gut* provider to your *fraa* one day."

Esther sank down low in her chair. *I can't believe* Mamm *said that! How embarrassing*, she thought. She noticed that Amos appeared to be a little embarrassed too.

Martha seemed oblivious to the slight tension that had descended over the table. "So, these gazebos, Amos. You make them out of wood?"

"Wood, but sometimes even vinyl," he said. "We use pressure treated wood that isn't affected by fungus or even termites. We don't use arsenic. It's all environmentally friendly."

As Amos went on at some length about the virtues of laminated posts versus other types of posts that crack, and the problem of damp wood, which is fixed by kiln drying, Esther found her mind drifting away. Her *mudder* was determined to find her a *mann.* Hannah was now married and Esther was the next *dochder* in line. Esther remembered the lengths her *mudder* had gone to, in her attempts to set up Hannah with the unsuitable David Yoder. *And now* Mamm*'s starting on me*, Esther thought with dismay.

"Esther!"

Esther looked up and saw all eyes on her. "Sorry, *Mamm*, what did you say?"

"I told Amos that you were the one who mainly prepared the dinner."

Esther went to protest, but her *mudder's* withering stare abruptly put a stop to that. "*Jah*, Esther's a *wunderbar* cook," Mrs. Miller continued. "Esther made the dessert, Cottage Pudding with butterscotch sauce. Wait until you taste it! She'll make some *mann* a good *fraa*."

Esther could have died with embarrassment right on the spot. *Oh well, I have to look on the bright side*, she thought, as her cheeks flushed red and her ears burned. *Wait until I tell Jacob. He'll have a good laugh over all this.*

Sadly, Mrs. Miller was still talking. "*Jah*, and Esther picked the celery herself. We still have plenty of celery growing, and there's still time to use it." Mrs.

Miller winked at Amos before she signaled to Rebecca and Martha to help her clear the plates.

It's going from bad to worse, Esther thought. *Could* Mamm *be any more obvious?* Esther knew that some communities had mason jars of cut celery on tables at the weddings. While her community didn't follow this practice, the fact that it was a well known tradition in other communities was enough to make her absolutely mortified that her *mudder* was alluding to the subject of marriage to Amos.

Esther stole a glance at Amos and saw that he was shifting uncomfortably in his seat. *I hope he doesn't think I'm attracted to him*, she thought with growing alarm. *What am I going to do?*

The dinner went downhill from there. Esther looked to her *daed* for help, but it appeared that he had given up trying to fight his *fraa's* matchmaking ways. Even Martha and Rebecca clearly were appalled at their *mudder's* efforts, as they kept shooting Esther sympathetic looks.

After Amos finally left, none too soon for Esther, Mrs. Miller gave the girls mending to do, and then went out on the porch to talk to her husband. As it was a warm night, all the windows were open, and Esther figured that her parents had forgotten that one fact, as their voices carried freely into where Esther, Martha, Rebecca, and Mary sat.

"You were no help tonight, Abraham," their *mudder* scolded him.

Their *daed* simply laughed. "Rachel, you will not make a match of Amos and Esther. You're wasting your time. Besides, isn't it time you forgave the Hostetlers? Hannah is already married to Noah."

The three girls looked at each other, while their *mudder* snorted. "*Nee*, I tell you. I will not have another of my *dochders* marry one of the Hostetler *familye*. *Nee*. Esther and Amos *will* be married, Abraham. You mark my words!"

As Abraham let out a well-worn and lengthy sigh of resignation, Martha whispered to Esther, "*Mamm* thinks you're going to marry Jacob. See, we all thought you were."

"What are you going to do?" Martha later asked her *schweschder*, when the three girls were playing Scrabble and their parents were out of earshot, reading the Bible in the kitchen.

Esther threw her hands in the air. "What can I do? There's nothing I can do. *Mamm* won't stop—she'll keep inviting Amos for dinner and trying to push me with him. Remember how she was with Hannah and David Yoder? The only thing that'll stop her is if Amos starts dating someone else."

"There's one other thing that will stop her, Esther." Martha placed a letter tile at the bottom of a row. "*Mamm* will stop matchmaking if you start dating someone."

"Don't be silly, Martha," Rebecca piped up. "Esther doesn't like anyone."

Nevertheless, Martha's words planted a small seed of an idea in Esther's mind, and as she lay in bed that night thinking over her problem, that small seed grew.

Chapter Four

Esther drove the *familye* buggy through a heavy haze, which was blocking the early morning sun from view. The shafts of sunlight found their way eerily through the mist, striking Esther with a lingering feeling of uneasiness. The air was heavy and still. The atmosphere sparkled with the promise of something about to happen. *What could possibly happen?* Esther thought. *I'm just a Plain girl about to ask a friend a favor.* Nevertheless, she could not shake the worrying feeling that, somehow, this day would change her life.

Esther intended to arrive early to catch Jacob before he was heavily involved in his chores. She drove her horse along the road, past recently harvested, bare yellow fields, as well as lush, green pastures where cattle grazed contentedly. The Hostetlers' farm was set amidst gently rolling hills, and the *haus* was flanked by a row of tall trees. There were so many barns that Esther didn't know quite which one to head for, but Jacob must have heard her coming as he waved to her from in front of one of the smaller white barns.

"*Hiya*, Jacob," she said, as he came over and held her horse's bridle.

"*Guten mariye*, Esther. What are you doing here?"

Esther suddenly felt nervous, and climbed down from the buggy to speak to Jacob. "I can't stay. I won't keep you from your work. I've just come to ask you for a favor."

Jacob looked at her quizzically.

"*Mamm's* trying to match me with Amos Troyer," she began.

"Amos?" Jacob interrupted her. "That good-looking *mann*?"

Esther nodded. "*Jah*."

Jacob frowned. "So, you think he's good-looking?"

"Well, *jah*, but that's not the point." Esther wondered why Jacob was looking a little annoyed.

Jacob let go of the horse's bridle and crossed his arms over his chest. "Have you come to tell me that you're dating Amos Troyer?"

"*Nee*, Jacob. I came to tell you that my *mudder* wants me to date Amos, but I don't want to." Esther noted that Jacob looked relieved. He was sure acting weird. *Perhaps he doesn't think Amos is suited to me*, she thought. "Anyway," she continued, "*Mamm* has her heart set on me dating Amos, so last night I came up with an idea. Would you mind if we pretended that we were dating?"

Jacob looked thunderstruck. "What, what," he stammered. "You want me to pretend that the two of us are dating? Each other?"

Suddenly the idea didn't seem such a good one to Esther. "Oh it sounds so silly when you say it, Jacob. I just thought it was the only way to stop *Mamm*. You have no idea how bad she was, when she tried to push Hannah and David Yoder together. Forget it. It's a silly idea." Esther made to get back into the buggy, but Jacob put his hand on her arm.

"Wait a moment. Let me get this straight. You want me to pretend that I'm dating you, to keep Amos Troyer away from you and to prevent your *mudder* trying to match up the two of you?"

Esther nodded. "Jacob, I'm really desperate."

"Oh *denki*, Esther!" His tone was highly offended.

Esther shook her head with irritation. "*Nee*, Jacob, why do you have to be so difficult? You know what I mean."

Jacob appeared to be thinking things over. "All right, I'll pretend that we're dating. Who will know the truth?"

"You, me, and *Gott*." Esther smiled. "*Denki* so much, Jacob. That's really *gut* of you. I don't know what I'd do without you. You're a *gut* friend." A thought occurred to Esther. "Oh, but I don't want to get in the way if you're interested in a girl."

Jacob rubbed his chin.

Esther fought the urge to stomp her foot. "Well, are you?"

"Am I what?"

Esther let out a loud sigh of frustration. "I don't want to pretend I'm dating you if you're interested in a girl. Are you?"

Jacob leaned back against the old, wooden fence post. "No need to worry, Esther. My love life won't suffer from pretending I'm dating you."

Esther looked at Jacob through narrowed eyes. Not only had he not directly answered her question, he appeared to be having a private joke with himself. Was there something he wasn't telling her?

"Anyway," she continued, "when you find a girl you want to date, we can break off our pretend dating."

"And we'll stop pretending if you want to date someone too, obviously," Jacob said.

"Don't be silly, Jacob! I don't want to date anyone."

Jacob simply raised his eyebrows. "Have you really thought this through, Esther? I don't know if we'll convince anyone, not after a while. And don't forget that all secrets come to light. *For nothing is secret, that shall not be made manifest; neither any thing hid, that shall not be known and come abroad.*"

"Oh, don't be so *Scripture smart*, Jacob." She gave him a playful tap on the arm. "*Denki* so much for helping me."

On the drive back to her *haus*, Esther worried about her plan. Sure, Jacob had agreed, but would people believe them? Her younger sisters would think it strange. Her *mudder* was the one she had to convince, after all. She was the matchmaker. Nevertheless, Esther had made up her mind to tell Hannah.

Jacob thought Esther's plan was a little unusual, and he wondered about her motivation. A large part of him hoped it was because Esther had feelings for him, although he was sure that she wasn't aware of those feelings. At least, she had never shown any indication that she was. Jacob feared that Esther would always see him just as her *gut* friend.

Still, this plan of Esther's afforded Jacob a window of opportunity. In fact, it was likely a blessing from *Gott*. Goodness knows that Jacob had often prayed to *Gott* about his feelings for Esther. If Esther enjoyed their time together, pretending to be a dating couple, perhaps she would finally start to see Jacob as more than just a *gut* friend.

He was also concerned about Amos Troyer. Jacob was only too well aware that Amos, despite his young age, already owned his own successful construction business. What's more, he was handsome, and all the girls flocked around him. Jacob sighed. Sure, Esther had said she wasn't interested in Amos, but then again, she didn't seem much interested in him, either. How could he compete with the accomplished Amos Troyer?

Chapter Five

Esther sat at the kitchen table, wringing her hands. She didn't want to lie. It was against her nature, and she hoped *Gott* would not be angry with her. Yet surely *Gott* could see how difficult her *mudder* was making her life, by trying to drive her to be Amos Troyer's *fraa*. The ministers were always telling people at church to hand their burdens over to *Gott*. Perhaps she should have prayed and let *Gott* sort it out for her, but pretending that she and Jacob were dating had seemed like a *gut* idea at the time. What could go wrong?

Esther studied the grain in the old, white oak table. People thought wood was simply plain, she thought absently, but she always marveled at the different patterns and the textures. Oak was somewhat rough to the touch. This table, which had belonged to her *Grossdawdi* and *Grossmammi*, had prominent rays of silver grain. Other woods, such as maple, had tight, strong curls in the grain, and her favorite, the elm, often had patterns of fascinating swirls. Esther smiled to herself. *That's what comes from being the* dochder *of a woodworker*, she thought.

Esther's parents joined her at the table. She could see they were puzzled as to what she had to say. Esther had no doubt that Martha and Rebecca would be able to overhear the upcoming conversation as they were in the living room, but she thought it would be better this way. It would save her having to tell the same lie to two sets of people. Esther winced as she remembered the minister's words that all sins would be found out. *But is pretending that I'm dating Jacob a sin?* Esther wondered. She thought some more. *Nee, but telling lies about it likely is.* She sent up a silent prayer to *Gott* to ask His forgiveness for what she felt was a necessary deception.

"*Datt*, *Mamm*, it's likely that Jacob and I will be going on a buggy ride together." She looked down at her hands, happy that her words, at least, were truth, if not her intention.

Her *vadder* beamed. "*Wunderbar*!" Mr. Miller had never held resentment against the Hostetler *familye*. In fact, Noah Hostetler worked for him in his furniture making business, the workshop of which was behind the Millers' *haus*.

Her *mudder* did not share his enthusiasm. "*Ach*, not another Hostetler boy! And what's wrong with Amos Troyer? Such a nice boy, and such a nice *familye*."

Her *daed* came to her rescue. "Now, Rachel, Hannah's very happy with Noah."

"*Jah*, that she is." Her mother's words agreed, but

her expression didn't. Her face was as black as a thundercloud.

Esther figured that her *mudder* had come to terms with one of her *dochders* marrying a Hostetler, but wasn't so happy with the possibility of another, to say the least. Her *mudder* still held resentment in her heart for Noah Hostetler accidentally causing the injuries to her and her *schweschders.*

The next morning, after Esther fed the chickens and prepared pancakes, eggs, and fried potatoes for everyone's breakfast, she headed to Hannah's *haus.* Hannah's husband, Noah, was already at her *daed's* furniture workshop, so she knew they would have privacy.

Esther was looking forward to having a good talk to her older *schweschder*, Hannah. The two of them were close and, in the days before Hannah married Noah, they would talk for hours most nights. Esther missed their talks.

It was a beautiful day, and Esther marveled at *Gott's* creation. Walking seemed to help her back too, as it ached less after a walk. The rising sun cast a golden glow over the fields, and colorful wildflowers swayed gently in the breeze, dispersing scents of cinnamon and lemon.

Esther smiled as Hannah's little *haus* came into view. It was white with a gray roof, and no front garden to speak of, but Hannah would soon have the front garden as well established as the existing back garden. She had already made a good start on the vegetable garden to the side of the *haus.* The *haus* had a large garage that Noah had already converted to a workshop, as well as a large field for their buggy horse.

"Esther, *wilkom*!" Hannah ushered her into her little *haus*. "*Kaffi*?"

"*Jah*, that would be *gut*, *denki*." Esther wished it were winter. In winter, *kaffi* was warm and cheering, as were wood fires. No matter what happened in winter, one could always be comforted by a pot of *kaffi* and a welcome fire. Still, the highly polished wooden floors in the *haus* were welcoming. Esther loved timber. If she had been a *mann*, she would have worked for her *daed* making fine, wooden furniture.

Hannah's voice broke into Esther's daydreaming. "Are you hungry? I was about to eat some *scrapple*."

"*Jah*, *denki*. Where's your new puppy?"

Hannah laughed. "Annie's asleep in Noah's workshop. Don't wake her up. She's just like a *boppli*. I'm always relieved when she's asleep. I didn't know that beagles were so energetic."

Esther laughed too, glad that Hannah finally had her own puppy. Their *mudder* had forbidden them to have pets, as she said that all animals must earn their keep.

Esther looked around the little room. The table was in the middle of the kitchen. Esther once again found herself looking at timber, this time, the cabinet doors, which were of a rich, red oak. The aroma of *kaffi* and cornmeal filled the air. The room was small, but welcoming and happy. Esther saw that Hannah was glowing, and wondered if she would ever find happiness with a *mann*.

Hannah nodded to the back door. "Let's eat outside, on such a beautiful day."

Esther followed Hannah outside and sat down on a green metal seat, at a small, plain metal table. The *haus*, while white timber at the front, was brick at the back, with shutters on each of the windows. English roses infused the air with their heady fragrance, and an old, white vinyl arbor next to where Esther was sitting was almost collapsing with the weight of the abundant orange flowers of an old trumpet vine.

Hannah followed Esther's gaze. "Noah will have to prune that soon," she said, before placing a steaming mug of *kaffi* and a bowl of scrapple in front of Esther. "What's up? You're very quiet today. Is everything all right?"

Esther took a sip of *kaffi* and shrugged. "*Nee*, *jah*, oh I don't know. *Mamm's* trying to do her matchmaking thing with me and Amos Troyer."

Hannah laughed. "Amos? He's good-looking, and seems nice."

Esther snorted rudely. "You didn't think it was so funny when you were on the receiving end of *Mamm's* matchmaking efforts, Hannah." Esther's tone held accusation.

Hannah sobered somewhat. "True, I see what you mean. I take it you don't like Amos then?"

Esther shook her head. "*Nee*. He's nice enough and all, it's just that—well, there's no spark. Do you know what I mean?"

Hannah nodded.

"I know what the bishop and the ministers say," Esther continued, "that we need a husband who has humility, is a hard worker and a *gut* provider, but they never say anything about attraction. I'm not going to marry a *mann* I'm not attracted to."

"Fair enough." Hannah shrugged. "Look, do you want to help me with the laundry? I was just about to finish washing the whites."

Esther nodded and they both stood up. Esther followed Hannah to the laundry room. "Do you feel the leading of *Der Herr* for any young man in particular?" Hannah asked.

"Well, I hadn't actually thought about getting married at all. It's just that when *Mamm* invited Amos for dinner, that I—" Esther's words were cut off by Hannah pulling the cord to start the little diesel motor on the old Maytag wringer washer.

"It's very loud."

Hannah turned to Esther. "What did you say?"

Esther moved closer to Hannah and nearly tripped over the exhaust pipe running out the window. "It's loud!" she yelled.

Both girls laughed.

Hannah poured buckets of hot water into the tub and added soap, and then bent down to turn on the knob at the front to activate the agitator. Once the water was swirling, she added the clothes.

Esther stood by, watching. She wanted to talk to Hannah, but there was no point trying to speak over the sound of the motor. The sight of the wringer reminded her that she had better hurry home and help her *mudder* with the laundry.

Hannah turned off the agitator, activated the safety release on the wringer, turned on the wringer, and then fed one item of clothing through the wringer at a time. All the while, Esther stood silently by. She wanted to have Hannah's undivided attention when she told her about the plot she had hatched with Jacob, or rather, the plan she had forced on Jacob. *He did seem quite willing though*, she thought.

When the machine pumped the dirty water out into a tall, fiberglass laundry tub, Esther exclaimed in surprise. "I didn't know this old model had a pump, Hannah! That's *gut*."

Hannah laughed, and yelled back, "*Jah*. It works better than it looks."

"That'll be *gut* when you're washing piles of diapers."

"*Ach*!" Hannah playfully hit Esther with a wrung-out shirt.

"I'm all wet now!" Esther said in mock horror, shaking droplets of water from her dress.

"Serves you right." Hannah laughed, and went back to wringing clothes.

Esther watched as Hannah poured more buckets of hot water into the tub for the rinse. "Do you want me to help?"

"*Nee*, Esther, not with your back. You're not supposed to lift anything heavy."

"My back feels okay now though."

"*Nee*," Hannah scolded. "Remember that the *dok-*

tor said that your back would feel *gut* long before it's healed? I did damage to my leg by walking on it much more than I should've."

Esther nodded as Hannah placed all the clothes back in the tub, added fabric softener, and turned on the agitator again, pushing the clothes down with a plunger to submerge them under the hot water. This time, she swung the wringer arm around and wrung out the clothes into the laundry basket.

When Esther handed her a white shirt, Hannah said, "*Nee*, I don't wring out the white shirts. I let them dry on the line—it saves ironing."

"I wish *Mamm* thought like you do," Esther said. "It takes me forever to iron all the wrinkled dresses, and *Mamm's* too fond of that horrible, old gas iron to replace it. I'm sure it's going to explode one day soon. When I marry, I'm going to hang all the dresses and shirts on the line without wringing them first to save me a lot of ironing."

Hannah turned to her with a smile. "I thought you weren't getting married."

Esther smiled. "Oh Hannah, that reminds me. I have something to tell you. Wait 'til we're hanging out the washing, though."

Hannah carried out the laundry basket into the summer sun, and then turned the crank to bring in the double-lined clothesline. It was a lovely day for washing. The warm breeze would dry the washing quickly and infuse the clothes with the scent of lavender and the fruity scent of the Nanho Blue Butterfly Bushes growing nearby. True to their name, butterflies were clustering around the Nanho Blue bushes, and spilling over onto the nearby lavenders. Esther stopped for a moment to look at the butterflies, some in colors of brilliant blues and others, reddish orange-brown with black spots.

Esther picked up a shirt to pin on the line. "Hannah, you know what *Mamm's* like with matchmaking."

"Hmm," Hannah replied, busily pinning clothes.

"*Mamm* wants me to marry Amos."

"Hmm." Hannah pinned another shirt to the line.

"So Jacob and I are going to pretend that we're dating."

Hannah stopped pinning clothes and turned to Esther. "What? Are you serious?"

Esther was taken aback. "Why? Don't you think it's a *gut* idea?"

Hannah stood there, and dropped a wet shirt back in the basket. "Whose idea was it?"

"Why, mine of course. I told Jacob that *Mamm* was trying to matchmake me with Amos Troyer and asked him if he'd pretend to be dating me."

Hannah took the shirt that Esther was about to pin from her. "Look, Esther, Jacob really likes you. Don't give him false hope! Don't lead him on."

Esther shook her head. "*Nee*, Hannah, it's not like that. Jacob and I are just friends." *Why do I spend all my time telling everyone that Jacob and I are just friends?* she thought, somewhat crossly.

Chapter Six

Esther awoke suddenly in the night.

She heard hushed voices, and the voices were coming from downstairs. Maybe it was morning, she thought, and she had slept in. She slipped from her bed and crossed the room to the window, where she drew the blinds. It was still dark outside, but in the distance, she could see billowing black smoke silhouetted by a red haze.

Something was wrong. She stepped away from the window and quickly got dressed, trying to ignore the thudding of her heart. Then she hurried downstairs.

Her *mudder* was in the kitchen. "*Mamm*," she asked, "what's happened? I saw fire in the distance."

"It's the Troyers. Their house caught fire in the night and nothing remains of it, only ashes."

Esther gasped. "Is everyone all right?"

"I believe so, but your father is going to find out."

Mrs. Miller pushed past Esther to answer a knock at the door, with Esther hard on her heels. It was

Mary. "What's happened?" she asked urgently. "I heard fire trucks."

"The Troyers' house is on fire," Esther told her.

Mary twisted her hands together, her eyes wide with alarm. "Is everyone all right?" Mary said.

"My husband has just gone to find out," Mrs. Miller told her.

Martha and Rebecca hurried down the stairs. "What's wrong?" they asked in unison.

Mrs. Miller folded her arms over her chest. "This is the third time I've had to tell someone. The Troyers' house burned down."

"Is everyone all right?" Martha said.

"I believe so, but we won't know for sure until your father gets home," Mrs. Miller said.

"None of us are going to be able to sleep. I'll make us all some hot chocolate," Esther said.

Soon they were all sitting around the kitchen table sipping hot chocolate. Esther usually loved sitting with her *familye*, but now her stomach clenched. She hoped the Troyers would be all right.

Everyone was on their second cup of hot chocolate when Mr. Miller returned, his face flushed. He raced through the door and went straight to Mrs. Miller, not acknowledging his daughters or Mary. "No one is hurt," he said, "but there's nothing left of the house or any of the contents. There's nothing left to be found."

"Where are they all going to stay?" Mrs. Miller asked him. Without waiting for him to respond, she added, "Lizzie Troyer can stay with us."

"The bishop said he was going to find somewhere

for them to stay," Mr. Miller said. He would have said more but Mrs. Miller cut him off once more.

"Go now Abraham, and tell them that we can take on Lizzie."

Mr. Miller left, taking with him the awful odor of singed hair and ash. Esther wondered how close her father had gotten to the fire and it worried her. She was also worried by her mother's offer to have Lizzie Troyer stay. Why Lizzie and not her parents? Or one or all of Lizzie's little *schweschders*?

Nee, Esther was certain that her mother wanted Lizzie there so Amos could visit. Esther hoped she wasn't being unkind, but she was sure her mother was plotting once more.

"Well, don't just stand there, girls," Mrs. Miller snapped. "Go and prepare somewhere for Lizzie to stay."

"Where would you like her to stay?" Esther asked.

Mrs. Miller frowned deeply. "She can stay with Mary in the *grossmammi haus*. It has an extra bedroom. That's all right, isn't it, Mary?"

"Of course," Mary said. "I'll be glad of the company. It's lovely having you all for company, but when I go to bed at night, there's no one there. I'm not used to being alone and it will be nice to have someone else around. I don't really know Lizzie well. What is she like? I know her brother Amos is pleasant enough and I have met Lizzie at the meetings and I've met all her younger sisters, but I haven't spoken to her in any depth. I do hope we'll get on. Yes, I'm sure we will."

When Mary finally stopped to draw breath, Mrs.

Miller pointed to the door. "My husband and Lizzie could be here at any minute, and I have no doubt Lizzie will be tired and upset. We need to prepare her room for her now."

Esther, Martha, Rebecca, and Mary all followed Mrs. Miller to the *grossmammi haus*. Esther hadn't seen the second bedroom there for some time and she was pleased to see it was tidy and clean, free of stored items.

"We will have to attend to the bed," Mrs. Miller said.

Esther knew that by *we*, Mrs. Miller meant Esther or one of her sisters would have to attend to the bed, so she set about getting the bed ready for Lizzie. When she had finished, she turned to her mother. "Is there anything else that Lizzie would need, do you think?"

Her mother appeared to be at a loss. "I don't know. She's Amos's older sister so she is not a young woman. Let this be a lesson to you, girls. Lizzie has not found a husband and so she is alone. She has to come and stay with us simply because she doesn't have a husband who could take her somewhere."

Esther thought her mother's logic was rather faulty. After all, Lizzie's parents had to find somewhere to stay, but she knew her mother took any opportunity to espouse the disadvantages of being a single woman.

Mrs. Miller was still speaking. "I know young girls of today have fanciful notions of love, but if a man is interested in you, then why not marry him? It will all work out. Sometimes I think girls of today are too fussy. They forget they themselves have shortcomings. Yet girls of today only look at the man's shortcomings and not his good qualities."

Esther squirmed as her mother was looking straight at her.

"Lizzie is not a young woman and she is past the age for *kinner*."

Martha dared to speak. "She's not that old, *Mamm*. She could have *kinner* if she wanted them."

Mrs. Miller clucked her tongue. "There is more to having *kinner* simply than wanting them, Martha," she said sternly. "Let this be a lesson to you and a reminder every time you see Lizzie. Lizzie is ten years older than Amos and is not married. I'm sure boys were interested in her when she was younger, but she no doubt found fault with them, just as some do."

With that, Mrs. Miller turned her gaze to Esther. "It's not *gut* to get to a certain age and not be married. Yes, you think you have all the time in the world, but you don't. Mark my words, that time will fly away and you'll find yourself an unmarried spinster just like Lizzie." With that, Mrs. Miller stormed out of the *grossmammi haus*.

The girls exchanged glances and followed her. They hadn't been back at the house long when Mr. Miller returned with Lizzie.

Esther, of course, knew Lizzie well having grown up in the same community as Lizzie. However, she had never taken to her. While Amos was pleasant enough, Lizzie had always been something of a gossip. Still, her heart went out to Lizzie at such a time as this.

Mrs. Miller greeted Lizzie warmly. "How are your parents, Elmer and Lavina?"

"They're fine, *denki*. Everyone escaped the fire."

"And Amos is *gut* too?" Mrs. Miller asked with a sidelong glance at Esther.

"*Jah*, he's helping the *menner* with the fire."

"And your younger *schweschders*, are they all right too?"

Lizzie nodded. "Everyone is all right. It's just the house has burned to the ground."

"We have prepared a room for you in the *gross-mammi haus* with Mary here," Mrs. Miller said.

Esther judged from the looks that Lizzie gave Mary that she wasn't too pleased with the arrangements.

"*Denki* for taking me in, Mrs. Miller. It is so kind of you." To Mary, she said, "I won't be any trouble. I like to keep to myself and I'm not fond of chatter."

It was all Esther could do not to gasp. She thought that rather rude of Lizzie. Surely her words were a barely veiled reference to Mary's nonstop talking.

"I'm sure you'd like a nice cup of meadow tea to settle your nerves," Mrs. Miller said. "Or perhaps chamomile tea would be better."

"*Jah, denki*. Chamomile tea would be nice," Lizzie said, shooting a glare Mary's way.

Mrs. Miller showed Lizzie into the living room and said goodbye to Mr. Miller who left once more to help with the fire. She soon returned with chamomile tea and set it in front of all the girls. Esther was half expecting to be dismissed to her bedroom so she was relieved that she wasn't.

"So what is the situation with your house?" Mrs. Miller asked Lizzie.

"The firefighters said it was a chimney fire," she said. "It is an old house, built in the 1800s."

Mrs. Miller clicked her tongue. "It is good that *Der Herr* saw fit to spare you and your *familye*."

Lizzie sipped her chamomile tea and did not respond.

"Were you able to save any of your furniture?" Mrs. Miller asked.

Lizzie shook her head. "*Nee*. It all happened so fast."

"Well, you are *wilkom* to stay with us. Do you know where the rest of your *familye* will be staying?"

Lizzie shook her head. "I'm not certain yet."

"I'm sure the rest of your *familye* won't stay too far away, and then Amos can come and visit you whenever he likes."

It was all Esther could do not to groan aloud. She was right—while her mother would have taken in a member of the Troyer family under any circumstances, the reason she chose Lizzie in particular was now obvious.

Chapter Seven

Esther had planned to drive Mary to the Yoders' farm the following day to visit Pirate, the dog Mary had found but which Mrs. Miller had refused to allow her to keep. That was no surprise—Mrs. Miller intensely disliked pets. She said an animal could not be allowed unless it paid its way. She always protested that it wasn't pets as such that she disliked, but the cost of useless pets, as she called them.

Mary had been sad, but David Yoder, Jessie Yoder's brother, had at once taken a liking to the dog and had taken him in. His mother, Beth Yoder, Mrs. Miller's closest friend, had allowed the dog to stay once she saw that he was frightened of all her cats. Although Mrs. Miller and Beth Yoder were best friends, Mrs. Miller certainly didn't share Beth Yoder's liking for pets.

Unfortunately for Esther, today Mrs. Miller had insisted she take along Lizzie Troyer. Esther's parents were over at the burned house site today to see what they could do to help. Of course, Esther's heart went out to Lizzie because she had lost her home, but Lizzie seemed disapproving of everything she did and made it abundantly clear she didn't like Mary's talkative nature. Esther wished her mother had taken in one if not all of Lizzie's younger sisters instead of Lizzie. That would certainly be better than the disapproving Lizzie.

Esther shook her head to clear her thoughts. She felt mean-spirited thinking such things about Lizzie when, after all, she had just lost her home.

Esther was also concerned because it was clear to her that her mother had taken in Lizzie simply because her mother wanted her to date Lizzie's brother, Amos.

As soon as Esther picked up the reins, Lizzie spoke. "Wasn't your sister interested in David Yoder once, Esther?"

"*Nee*," Esther said more forcefully than she intended. "He might have been interested in Hannah, but Hannah was certainly not interested in him."

Lizzie piped up. "I'm surprised your mother allowed Hannah to marry Noah. After all, he caused the accident that nearly killed you and your sisters."

Oh, so that's the way it's going to be, Esther thought. Aloud she said, "*Gott* wants us to forgive."

"Forgiving is one thing, but your mother surely had every right to disapprove of the marriage," Lizzie pressed on.

Esther looked over her shoulder to see a stern look on Lizzie's face.

"Oh, did David Yoder have a crush on Hannah?" Mary asked. "I didn't know David had a crush on Hannah. He didn't tell me that. Of course David doesn't tell me everything. I just didn't think Hannah would be his type. Then again, I don't know what David's type would be. David isn't seeing anyone now, is he? I mean, it's none of my business, but I haven't seen him with any of the girls. He seems a private person, doesn't he? Not that I know because I haven't been in the community all that long as far as things go. He loves dogs though. Isn't that good? He takes very good care of Pirate. I'm glad we can share Pirate because your mother won't let me have him, Esther. But please don't think I'm complaining about your mother. She's a lovely woman and it's lovely to be helping her. It's just that I don't know what would have happened if David hadn't adopted Pirate."

"Look at the ducks," Lizzie said in a loud voice.

"Where?" Esther asked automatically, but a split second later realized Lizzie had only said that to stop Mary talking. Esther knew by now that Mary talked quickly and at length only when she was nervous, and obviously Lizzie was making Mary quite nervous.

"So what do you think of my brother?" Lizzie asked Esther, but Mary interrupted her.

"I don't see any ducks? Where were they? Did they fly out of the pond? I didn't see them. If you see them again, will you point them out to me?"

Lizzie ignored her and pushed on. "Esther, I asked *you* what you thought of my brother."

"He seems a nice person," Esther said.

"You're not interested in anyone else, are you?"

"Actually, I'm seeing Jacob Hostetler," Esther said.

That brought a sharp intake of breath from Lizzie. "Not another Hostetler? Haven't you thought of your *mudder*? It would break her heart if another of her *dochders* married another Hostetler! Why, whatever would she say? Does she know?"

"*Jah*, she knows," Esther said. She was quite irritated by Lizzie. But then again, Lizzie had suffered a terrible experience and it was Esther's job to make her feel better. Besides, Esther was at a loss as to how to respond.

"Surely you could find another suitable young *mann* to marry," Lizzie continued. "I'm sure my younger *bruder* is interested in you. He's a good *mann* and has his own business. It would make your *mudder* happy. Don't make the same mistake I did, Esther."

"What mistake is that?" Esther asked her, guiding the horse over to the side of the road as a large truck roared past. The horse barely flinched. He was an older horse experienced with trucks. Esther clicked him on once the truck had passed.

"Look how old I am and I don't have any *kinner*. I wanted *kinner* and I was never interested in a man. Although several *menner* were interested in me, I was not interested in any of them. I didn't realize my life would flash by and I would remain unmarried at my age."

Esther nodded slowly. Martha was right—Lizzie wasn't all that old and could have children if she wanted. Esther thought Lizzie was being overly dramatic.

Lizzie pushed on. "Why, when I was eighteen, I could have married then, but I thought I was too young, despite my mother telling me I wasn't. I was a silly, foolish, headstrong girl. I had more opportunities to marry once again when I was twenty, but I didn't. I always thought someone would come along, someone for whom I would have romantic feelings, but I never did. Do you see what I mean?"

Esther continued to nod.

"So what I'm saying is, Esther, I know you think my words might not be true, but they are. Don't wait to have romantic feelings for a boy. You should marry the first one who shows interest in you, because *Gott* will make it all work out."

"But I was brought up to believe that *Gott* has a man and a woman already chosen for each other," Esther said.

The cold silence that descended on the buggy was palpable. Finally, Lizzie spoke. "Yes, but that doesn't mean you will feel romantic feelings for that man, or I would have someone by now, wouldn't I? That's surely logical, isn't it?"

"I suppose so," Esther said slowly and then added, "but I have romantic feelings for Jacob Hostetler." She felt bad lying, but she couldn't bear to listen to Lizzie's words any longer.

Fortunately for Esther, they had arrived at the Yoders' house. Esther jumped out of the buggy as fast as she could and tied her horse to the rail. Lizzie followed her, her face as black as a thundercloud. Mary jumped down from the buggy, seemingly oblivious to all the tension, and ran past the pair as Pirate ran to meet her.

"Pirate, Pirate!" she cried, throwing her arms around the dog's neck. Pirate stood up, planting his paws on Mary's shoulders and licking her face.

"Down, Pirate," David said. "Sorry, Mary. I have been training him, but he gets too excited when he sees you."

"What a dirty thing to do," Lizzie said. "Mary, wash your face at once."

Instead of being offended, Mary replied, "That wouldn't help. Pirate would only lick my face again and then I'd be washing my face again and again the whole time and not patting Pirate, which is what I came here to do. I've come here to see Pirate, you see. I can wash my face when I go back to the *gross-mammi haus*, otherwise I'd be washing my face every few seconds because he'd keep licking my face."

Esther noticed Lizzie had crossed her arms over her chest. It was plain to see Mary irritated her.

David Yoder came over to them. "*Hullo*, Esther." His greeting was polite but not warm. He turned to Lizzie. "I'm so sorry about what happened to your house. I'm sure we will be building your new one soon, so not to worry."

Lizzie beamed at him. "That's so kind of you, David."

Lizzie was a completely different person around David. In fact, Esther even wondered if Lizzie's tone had been flirtatious but then dismissed the notion. After all, she was eight to ten years his senior, Esther guessed. Esther noticed Mary was watching the exchange intently.

"Pirate is doing really well," David said to Mary.

Mary giggled. "Look, he's put on even more weight. You can't let him get too fat, David."

"I don't think he could ever get too fat because he's always so full of energy," David said with a laugh.

Esther had to admit David was certainly fond of that dog. She figured that anyone who liked dogs must be a nice person. She knew David had pursued Hannah, but that no doubt had been encouraged by her mother. Out of the context of Hannah, Esther was beginning to see David in a new light. Every time she took Mary over to see the dog, David seemed quite a nice person. She was a little wary of him as she'd heard he'd been seen with *Englisch* girls, but that was a long time ago.

Unfortunately, David did have one drawback, and that was his sister, Jessie. Jessie stalked over, her eyes narrowed. "What are you doing here, Esther?" she said, ignoring Mary and Lizzie.

Esther took a step backward. "I've brought Mary as I usually do."

"Jessie, haven't you noticed that Lizzie is here?" David said in a scolding tone.

"*Hullo*, Lizzie," Jessie said. "I am very sorry to hear about your house. I'm glad no one was hurt."

"*Denki*, Jessie," Lizzie said, but before she had

even finished speaking, Jessie stalked away wearing a sulky expression on her face.

Beth Yoder appeared at the door. She saw Lizzie and then hurried down and took her by the arm. "Oh you poor thing. *Der Herr* works in mysterious ways, that's for sure. Who can understand His ways? Well, I'm sure some good will come out of this. You must come inside right away." She led Lizzie away and then looked back over her shoulder. "You too, of course, Esther."

Esther was embarrassed but hurried after the pair, leaving Mary and David to play with an enthusiastic Pirate.

Beth Yoder opened the door for Lizzie and let it swing back toward Esther, who had to catch it with one hand.

I wonder what I've done to offend Mrs. Yoder? Esther thought.

"You two sit and I'll bring in the meadow tea. Relax," Mrs. Yoder said.

Lizzie and Esther sat in uncomfortable silence until Beth Yoder returned to the room with a tray of cups and a plate of whoopie pies in an assortment of chocolate, strawberry, gingerbread, pumpkin, and vanilla. Esther reached for the closest one and put it on her plate.

"Now, you must tell me all about the fire," Beth Yoder said to Lizzie. "What caused it?"

"The firefighters said it was a chimney fire," Lizzie said. Her hands trembled as she reached for a vanilla buttercream pie, and Esther felt terrible for having unkind thoughts toward her.

Lizzie took a bite out of the whoopie pie and a sip of the meadow tea before she continued. "The firefighters said it was probably because the house was built in the 1800s, but I don't know what that has to do with anything since my father cleaned out the chimney every year."

"But it's summer," Beth said. "Why did you have the fire on?"

Lizzie shook her head. "*Nee*, it wasn't that fire. It was the kitchen fire. We heat our water from the kitchen fire." She paused and then added, "Or we used to heat it that way, but I suppose my parents will use gas for the new *haus*."

Esther hadn't realized people in the community used coal or wood fires to heat their water. As far as she knew, everyone used propane or natural gas.

Beth Yoder made a clicking sound with her tongue. "I was thankful to hear that no one was hurt."

Lizzie nodded vigorously. "*Jah*. Houses can be replaced."

"And no doubt yours will be soon, so please don't worry," Beth said. "You need to keep up your strength. Here, have another whoopie pie, and can you stay for lunch?"

"*Denki*," Lizzie said.

Esther's heart sank. She was going to be stuck there for lunch with Lizzie and Beth, and no doubt the conversation would turn to the reason she shouldn't date Jacob Hostetler, and no doubt Beth Yoder would agree.

"Esther, would you please fetch Mary and David and tell them to come in for lunch?" Beth asked her.

As Esther left the room, Beth and Lizzie spoke in low voices and she heard her name mentioned. She hurried out the door. David and Mary were throwing sticks to Pirate. He wasn't consistent at fetching and they were laughing about the fact.

"Honestly, he does much better when you're not here," David said. "I think he's just excited to see you."

"It doesn't matter," Mary said. "He's a good dog and I'm happy to see him."

Esther walked over to them, noticing they hadn't seen her coming. She cleared her throat and they both spun around.

"David, your *mudder* has kindly invited us all to lunch. She asked that I fetch you for lunch now."

Both David and Mary looked pleased. Esther wondered if Mary had a little crush on David. It wasn't the first time she had thought that, but while David seemed to enjoy Mary's company, Esther didn't know if he saw Mary as anything more than a friend.

When Esther walked inside, Lizzie was sitting alone.

"How are you feeling today?" David asked her. "I know everyone was okay, but was anyone harmed at all?"

"Amos's eyebrows were singed because he kept

trying to go back in to save things," Lizzie said, "but my father stopped him."

Beth Yoder hurried in from the direction of the kitchen. "*Jah*, it's good that your father stopped him." She clasped her hands. "And this is so good that you are staying for lunch. We will have Hasenpfeffer. I've been marinating it for two days."

Mary muttered to herself and everyone looked at her. "What did you say?" Beth asked her.

"Nothing, nothing at all," Mary said.

Esther thought Mary had muttered to herself, "Poor little rabbits," but she couldn't be sure.

"Lizzie, my husband isn't joining us today because he's working at your house," Beth said. "Don't you worry, Lizzie. The *menner* will build your new house in no time. I know it was a nice old home, but your new house will be safe."

Lizzie nodded slowly. "*Jah*, that's what matters, safety not looks."

Beth nodded enthusiastically. "Now, Esther, would you help me with the meal?"

Esther followed Beth into the kitchen with some trepidation. She figured Beth was up to something. "So then Esther, how is your mother?"

"My mother is well, *denki*," she said.

"And is it true that you and Jacob are going on a buggy ride together?"

Esther gasped at Mrs. Yoder being so forthright. She looked down at the rabbit meat simmering in a frying pan in butter. "*Jah*," she said in a small voice.

"I do hope you're thinking of your poor mother's feelings," Beth continued.

Esther looked up. "*Jah*," she said again, at a complete loss as to what to say.

"Yes, your poor mother is still upset about Hannah marrying Noah Hostetler." Beth almost spat the words. "It must be breaking her heart to see you dating Jacob."

"*Mamm* has accepted Hannah and Noah marrying," Esther said, considering herself brave to speak out so boldly. "She knows Hannah is happy."

"But is your mother happy?" Beth said. She set down a pot of Dutch sour cream and turned around to look into Esther's eyes. "Young people often don't consider their parents."

Esther didn't know what to say, so just stood there. She was aware she was trembling.

After what seemed an age, Beth Yoder broke eye contact. "Then you had better go and fetch my daughter for lunch," she said. "Off you go. It's ready now."

The last thing in this world Esther wanted was to be alone with Jessie Yoder, but she had no choice. She found Jessie down by the barn, throwing stones against the barn wall. "Jessie," she called out. Jessie didn't turn around but stomped something under her foot. Esther finally had to walk right over to Jessie and tap her on the shoulder.

Jessie reeked of cigarette smoke. Esther realized that she hadn't been stomping on a stone but maybe a cigarette.

Jessie turned around. "*Jah*, what do you want?" Her tone was ice cold.

"Your mother sent me to fetch you for lunch."

Jessie's eyes narrowed even further until they formed tiny slits. "Does that mean you're staying for lunch too?"

"Yes, and Mary and Lizzie," Esther said. "Your mother is doing her best to make Lizzie feel better after her house burning down and all that."

Esther turned and hurried back to the house. She was worried Jessie would catch up with her and ask her probing questions about Jacob, but she didn't. Esther looked back over her shoulder to see if Jessie was following. She had paused by the peppermint growing beside the front pathway, and was crushing some leaves in her hands.

When Esther hurried into the house, everyone was sitting at the table and a huge bowl of Hasenpfeffer was in the middle of the table.

"Please sit down, girls," Beth said. They all bowed their heads for the silent prayer.

When Esther opened her eyes, Jessie was glaring at her. It quite unnerved her.

The talk at first was of Lizzie's house. "I'm going over there after lunch to see what I can do," David said, "if that's okay with you, *Mamm*?"

Beth Yoder waved one hand at him. "Of course. See what you can do to help the *menner*."

"I hope we can do something to help as well," Mary said. "It would be good to do something to help. Will there be a fundraising? We could also crochet or perhaps it will be a pie fundraising and we could help make pies."

She would have said more, but Beth Yoder cut her off. "Lizzie, where are your parents staying? I do think you told me, but I have forgotten already."

"My parents are staying with Levi and Susanna Lapp, and my younger *schweschders* are staying with Moses and Anna Fisher."

"They are all together?" Beth asked her.

Lizzie nodded.

"And Amos? Where is Amos staying?" Beth asked with a pointed look at Esther, who squirmed in her seat.

"Amos is staying with the widower, Wayne King," Lizzie said. "Mrs. Miller has kindly invited him over for dinner tonight."

Esther looked up sharply. That was the first she had heard of it. Her mother's plans were working out to her mother's liking, clearly.

"So David, have you found yourself a young *maidel* yet?" Lizzie asked him.

It was David's turn to squirm in his seat. He looked at his fork, on which tiny noodles were impaled. "*Nee, nee, nee*," he sputtered.

Lizzie seemed dissatisfied. "I was just telling Esther on the way here that you young people think you have all the time in the world, but you need to find someone while you are still young. Don't think you'll have more time to find someone, because that time will get away from you. Isn't that right, Beth?"

Esther thought Beth would agree, but she was surprised to see two red dots form on her cheeks. "That is usually the case, Lizzie, yes," Beth said slowly, "but it cannot be the wrong person. I would not like David to marry the wrong person."

Esther was surprised to see Beth's eyes stray to Mary. On their frequent visits when she had taken Mary to visit Pirate, Beth had never invited them inside. Not once had she even offered them a cup of meadow tea on the porch. Did Beth think something was going on between David and Mary, or was she simply overly concerned? And what was wrong with Mary? Esther was quite fond of Mary and now thought of her as one of her sisters. What could Beth's objection be, unless she had another girl in mind?

Lizzie seemed put out by that statement. "Don't encourage the young people so, Beth," she said. "They should not go running around with just anyone, but they do need to get married young. Don't you agree?"

"I do agree," Beth said, stabbing a piece of rabbit with unnecessary force, "but a wrong marriage would not be good."

"Yes, of course, yes, of course," Lizzie said, nodding vigorously. "We have all seen the wrong marriages in our community." She and Beth stared at Esther, and Esther realized they were talking about the marriage of Hannah and Noah. Esther was quite annoyed and couldn't wait to leave. She certainly didn't feel welcome there.

Throughout the debate, David and Mary had been conversing in low tones about Pirate.

"Honestly David, haven't you been listening to a word we have said?"

David looked up. "Sorry, *Mamm*."

Beth stood up to clear the table. "Mary, you have barely touched your Hasenpfeffer."

"I'm so sorry, Mrs. Yoder. I'm, um, allergic to rabbit." Mary looked around the room wildly, and Esther suppressed a giggle.

Esther stood up, intending to help Beth, but Lizzie said, "I'll help you, Beth. You stay here, Esther." A conspiratorial look passed between Beth and Lizzie, and Esther was certain they were going to talk about her. In fact, they had barely reached the kitchen door when she heard her name mentioned.

No one spoke. After a lengthy interval, Esther said, "Pirate is nice and shiny."

David looked pleased. "Yes, he eats a lot."

Mary waved one finger at him. "Mind you, it won't be good if he gets too fat."

David laughed. "Don't worry, Mary. He runs around too much to get fat. You don't need to worry about him. I look after him well."

"I know you do," Mary said.

Esther waited for her to say more but she didn't. She figured that meant Mary was comfortable around David because she certainly talked nonstop when she wasn't comfortable.

"It's a terrible thing that happened to the Troyers," David continued. "There will be a fundraiser very soon."

Esther was going to respond but Lizzie and Beth

returned. “Sawdust pie,” Beth said as she placed a large pie dish on the table.

“We don’t have sawdust pie in our community,” Mary said. “Mrs. Miller told me it looks like sawdust because of all the coconut, and there are a lot of lumber yards and mills around here full of sawdust, and the pie looks like them because of the coconut. It is a very nice pie, I must say.”

Esther wondered how Mary could say so many words without pausing for breath.

Lizzie sat down hard on her chair. “Idle words are not well spoken,” she said.

Esther tried to remember if that was a quote from the Bible, but she didn’t think it was. She figured Lizzie would never quote the Bible in public lest someone accused her of being Scripture smart for demonstrating her knowledge of the Bible. One thing was certain—Lizzie was being mean to Mary.

Much to Esther’s amazement, David spoke up. “Mary has a lot of interesting things to say,” he said, earning him a warning glance from his mother.

Lizzie’s face flushed beet red. Esther wondered if Lizzie had considered her words to be thinly veiled and was surprised that they were taken for what they indeed were. She sighed aloud. While it was certainly good to take in a neighbor in need, it was going to be hard when that neighbor in need was someone like Lizzie Troyer. To make matters worse, that night Esther had to sit through a dinner with Amos Troyer. She certainly wasn’t looking forward to it.

“And how have you been, Jessie?” Lizzie asked.

Esther had almost forgotten Jessie was at the table, as she hadn't spoken a word throughout the meal. "*Gut*, *denki*," was all she said while staring fixedly at her sawdust pie.

"Do you have a young *mann*?" Lizzie asked her.

"I will have soon," Jessie said through a mouthful of pie. She looked out of the corner of her eye at Esther.

Esther's stomach churned.

Chapter Eight

Esther put the horse in the field after rubbing him down. Then she hurried into the house to find her mother. She was in the kitchen, preparing dinner. "*Mamm*," Esther said, "did you tell anyone I was going on a buggy ride with Jacob?"

Her mother looked up. "What about a *hullo* for your mother?" she said icily.

"Sorry. *Hullo*, *Mamm*."

"*Hullo*, Esther."

Her mother didn't say anything else, so Esther asked her again.

Her mother looked up, her eyes narrowed. "What sort of question is that, Esther? Of course I didn't tell anyone. Who would I tell? It's not as if I'm happy about the fact."

Her mother looked about to snap at her again when she paused. "Perhaps I mentioned it to Beth Yoder, but I can't be sure. I don't think I did, but it's entirely possible. What of it?"

"Nothing, *Mamm*," Esther said meekly. "What can I do to help?"

Her mother gestured around the kitchen. "We're having Leber Kloese for dinner. We won't dice the celery and parsley until later. We will have flat rock pudding with maple syrup, and pineapple pie. Why don't you make some meadow tea for Lizzie and sit with her a while."

"*Jah*."

Esther had no desire to sit with Lizzie. Mary was sweeping the floors. Esther wished she could sweep the floors and leave Mary with Lizzie, but had to do what her mother had asked.

Rebecca and Martha were both asleep on the couches. The injuries made them tired, although they were well on their way to recovery. Esther was pleased that Rebecca was finally home from the hospital, and smiled at her sister's sleeping face.

Esther and Lizzie sat together, sipping meadow tea. Lizzie didn't say anything else about Amos or Jacob for that matter, much to Esther's relief.

When it was approaching time for dinner, Esther and Mary helped Mrs. Miller dice the onions, celery, and parsley, and shape the beef liver into balls. They wrapped the dough around them to form dumplings. Mrs. Miller had refused any help from Lizzie. "Are the dumplings ready to boil now?" Mary asked Esther.

"*Nee*, I think *Mamm* wants to wait until Amos comes," Esther said. "They might want to speak before dinner. I'm not sure when he's coming, though."

As she walked out to ask Mrs. Miller, Mr. Miller was showing Amos in.

"I'm so sorry about your house, Amos," Esther said, noting that his eyebrows were singed. Her heart went out to him.

"*Denki*, Esther," he said. "It is just as well that my business is in town and not at the farm."

"Yes, indeed." That hadn't even occurred to Esther. It would have been even worse for Amos if his whole business had gone up in smoke.

"You look well, Lizzie," Amos said to his sister.

"Yes, the Millers have been looking after me very well. How are our parents and our sisters?"

"They're all doing quite well," Amos said. "The bishop spent time with our parents today."

"You sit and chat with Amos while I go attend to the dinner," Mrs. Miller said. "It's almost ready."

Esther made to rise, but her mother waved her back down. "*Nee*. Mary and I can see to the dinner. You stay there."

It was all Esther could do not to roll her eyes. If only her mother would give up trying to match her with Amos, but matchmaking came naturally to Mrs. Miller and there was nothing anyone could do about it, not even Mr. Miller.

"So will you get gas heating in your new house?" Mr. Miller asked Amos.

Amos nodded. "*Jah*, the bishop has recommended it. It would certainly be safer. Besides, my parents might be worried about another chimney fire."

"We had lunch at Beth Yoder's today," Lizzie informed Amos.

"That's nice," he said absently.

"Jessie Yoder has her eyes on a young *mann,*" Lizzie said.

"Oh," was Amos's only response. He did not look at all interested, but on the other hand, Esther felt sick to the stomach.

Why would Lizzie say that? she wondered. *Does she want me to think that Jessie is seeing Jacob?* Lizzie's words made Esther uneasy.

There was a knock on the door. Mr. Miller opened it and Mr. and Mrs. Hershberger walked in. "It's lovely to see you, Amos and Lizzie," Mr. Hershberger said. "We've come about your house."

Amos shook hands with Mr. Hershberger. "*Denki* for your help," he said.

"We are going around to everyone telling them there's going to be a pie fundraiser," Mr. Hershberger said. "There will be an auction at some future date, but that will take time to organize, whereas it won't take long to organize a pie fundraiser. The ladies can spend tomorrow making the pies and the fundraiser can be the day after."

Mrs. Miller beamed. "*Wunderbar*," she said. "Esther, Mary, and I can make pies all day tomorrow."

"I can help too," Lizzie said.

Mrs. Miller waved one hand at her. "*Nee*, you need to rest after your ordeal. You can rest and speak with Rebecca and Martha."

Martha and Rebecca exchanged glances. Esther

wondered if they had been on the receiving end of one of Lizzie's talks. Esther was looking forward to a day of baking pies. No matter how hard the work, she was certain it would be better than listening to Lizzie telling her how unsuitable Jacob was or her advice on marriage.

"Where will the pie fundraiser be held?" Mr. Miller asked Mr. Hershberger.

"Those details haven't been finalized yet but we'll let everyone know soon," he said. "But for now, the more pies the better. We need as many pies as possible."

"We can make all sorts of pies, and lots of them," Mrs. Miller said.

"*Denki*," Amos said.

Mrs. Hershberger walked over and handed Lizzie a package. "There are some clothes in there that should fit you, Lizzie, and a prayer *kapp* and a bonnet."

"*Denki,*" Lizzie said.

"And we have left some clothes for you at Wayne King's," Mrs. Hershberger said to Amos. *"Mir hen Englischer bsuch ghadde."*

"You had non-Amish visitors?" Amos repeated.

Mrs. Hershberger nodded. "*Jah*. The *Englischers* have made plentiful donations of food."

"How kind of them," Amos said.

"In fact, the *Englischers* have donated heavy machinery and a driver to clear away the remains so the new house can be built," Mr. Hershberger said.

"How kind of them," Amos said again. This time, he beamed from ear to ear.

"Yes, they have been very kind and many of them have stopped by your house to make donations," Mr. Hershberger said. "Well, if you'll excuse us, we have to go on and tell everyone else. Good night, everyone. Good night, Abraham and Rachel."

"*Guten nacht*." Mr. Miller showed the Hershbergers to the door.

"I had better see to the Leber Kloese," Mrs. Miller said. "Come with me, Mary." She marched Mary out of the room. Mary was chattering nonstop, so Esther knew she was nervous.

"Did you have lunch at the Yoders' too?" Amos asked Esther.

"*Jah*." She shot him a small smile.

"That's *gut*," he said, looking at his feet.

Esther shifted in her seat. Amos was a nice person, but she wasn't able to speak with him. The conversation was jarring and there were always lots of awkward silences, unlike conversations with Jacob where everything flowed easily. It was entirely different with Amos.

Amos persisted in trying to make conversation. "It was good that your parents took in Lizzie."

"They were happy to do it. Your sister is most welcome," Esther said honestly. She smiled at Lizzie, but Lizzie did not return her smile. Esther could see Lizzie was up to something, but she had no idea what. What could she be plotting?

Esther shook her head to dispel her thoughts. *Maybe I'm just getting paranoid*, she thought.

Soon the table was laden under Leber Kloese,

sauerkraut, pickle relish, and vegetables. Everyone bowed their heads for the silent prayer and once again when Esther opened her eyes, Lizzie was staring straight at her. *If she dislikes me, why does she see me as a suitable* fraa *for her brother, Amos?* Esther asked herself.

The conversation over dinner was all about the fire. It had burned quickly, and no one had been able to save any clothes or their old books. *The Martyr's Mirror* that had belonged to Mr. Troyer's great grandfather was lost, as was their German Martin Luther Bible.

"We will raise enough funds not only to replace your house but your furniture and clothing as well," Mr. Miller said, "just like ten years ago when the Rabers' house was struck by lightning."

Later that night, Mary and Esther were helping Mrs. Miller in the kitchen, washing the dishes.

"I'm very tired. I might go back to my room now," Lizzie said.

"*Guten nacht*," Mrs. Miller said and Esther made to say goodnight too, but Lizzie beckoned to her.

"Esther, would you walk me to my room?"

"Yes, of course," Esther said, wondering why Lizzie would need to be walked to her room.

As soon as they were out of the house and onto the pathway to the *grossmammi haus*, Lizzie leaned closer to Esther. "My *bruder* likes you," she whispered.

Esther had no idea how to respond. She broke out into a cold sweat.

"Do you like my *bruder*?" Lizzie persisted.

"I am seeing Jacob Hostetler," Esther told Lizzie.

Lizzie muttered something that sounded to Esther suspiciously like Esther must be out of her mind. "But he is not suitable for you. Don't you understand that?" Lizzie hissed. "Your mother would be so sad if another of her daughters married a Hostetler. Why, the poor woman can scarcely bear it that Hannah married Noah."

"But it is my choice whom I marry," Esther said.

They had reached the *grossmammi haus*. "It's not good to be rude to your elders," Lizzie snapped.

"I'm sorry. I wasn't being rude; I was simply stating the truth," Esther said meekly. She held her breath, wondering what Lizzie's response would be.

Lizzie appeared to be thinking it over. Finally, she said, "I understand. I was a silly headstrong girl at your age too, but look where it got me. Now I'm alone and with no *kinner*. Is that what you want to happen to you?"

Esther shook her head. "No, but..."

Lizzie held up one hand. "*Nee*, there is no 'but.' I know you entertain foolish notions of this boy, but it would upset your mother so, and my brother is a good man, is he not?"

"Yes, he is a very good man," Esther agreed.

"Then why do you not wish to go on a buggy ride with my brother?"

"Because I'm going on a buggy ride with Jacob," Esther said.

With that, Lizzie stomped her foot and stormed into the *grossmammi haus*.

Chapter Nine

Mrs. Miller slammed pots and pans around all morning. Esther was half expecting her mother to forbid her to go on the buggy ride with Jacob. She knew her mother was furious with the idea, but Mr. Miller was always in favor of the Hostetlers and after all, Noah Hostetler worked for him. Hannah's marriage to Noah certainly hadn't softened Mrs. Miller's heart toward the Hostetlers.

Lizzie Troyer was still sulky over breakfast and barely afforded Esther a glance. "I'm so excited you're going on a buggy ride with Jacob this morning," Mary said rather unwisely, given the way Lizzie and Mrs. Miller felt about the situation. "How exciting. Where will you go on the buggy ride, Esther?" Before Esther could respond, Mary continued. "No one has ever asked me on a buggy ride. I wish someone would ask me on a buggy ride. I'm worried that I won't ever get married or have *kinner*."

"Don't be away long, Esther, you have work to do,"

Mrs. Miller snapped. "Those pies won't bake themselves, and we have a lot to make."

"Now Rachel, Esther can take as long as she likes," Mr. Miller said.

Esther noticed Lizzie had her mouth open to say something, but Mr. Miller's words stopped her.

Martha and Rebecca giggled, no doubt due to the tension at the table. "I'll go and wait for Jacob outside," Esther said as she beat a hasty retreat.

Esther sat on the porch step, waiting for Jacob to come. Every now and then she glanced anxiously over her shoulder, fearful that her mother or Lizzie would come and say something to upset her, maybe even prevent her from going on the buggy ride.

She looked at the washing line as a gust of wind swung her *vadder's* broadfall trousers high in the air. Maybe she should run over and unpin them. No, she wanted to leave with Jacob as soon as he arrived.

Esther then looked to her left and saw the rose bushes along the front fence. Some of them needed pruning. Maybe she should do it now. Esther rubbed her temples. *Nee*, she had to wait for Jacob to come. Esther put her hand down on the porch beside her and saw it needed sweeping. *Maybe I have time to sweep it before Jacob comes*, she thought.

No, this would not do at all. Everywhere Esther looked there was work to be done. She felt guilty going on a buggy ride with Jacob, but that's exactly what she would have to do, or her mother would apply more pressure for her to marry Amos. It was bad timing, to be sure, as she should be inside making pies or sweeping the porch, or pruning the roses, or taking the laundry inside, but she had said she would go on a buggy ride with Jacob and that's exactly what she intended to do.

Jacob had been so good to her to pretend that they were dating. She was glad she had such a friend as he. Right from childhood, the two of them had been close. They understood each other in a way most people didn't. It seemed like only last week that she had picked wild raspberries on the little lane to the pond, but it was years ago. How time had flown.

Esther clutched at her stomach. Was Lizzie right? Did the years go by in the twinkling of an eye? If she didn't marry Amos or some other *mann*, would she be here standing by the very porch where she was standing now, alone and unmarried, while her sisters were all married and with *kinner*? Hannah was already married and Esther was the next sister in line.

Lizzie certainly seemed sure the years passed by quickly. Esther had heard some of the women say their biological clocks were ticking and that they must get married soon, but Esther had paid it no mind. Those girls were in their mid twenties and Esther was not that old, but she did not want to get past the age for having *kinner*.

But could she live in a loveless marriage if she was simply friends with her husband like some women said they were?

Esther took a deep breath and let it out slowly. There was so much thinking she had to do, but she didn't have time to think. Every night she was asleep as soon as her head hit the pillow, and as soon as she awoke in the morning it was time to go downstairs and make *kaffi* and breakfast. *Nee*, Esther craved time to herself, but she didn't get any, and it was worse now that Lizzie was there. Esther felt that Lizzie was already making her life difficult and she had only just arrived. What was she to do?

Esther looked to the horizon behind the rolling green hills and saw storm clouds gathering. Maybe that's why she was so tense. Esther enjoyed storms, but sometimes they made her uneasy. She did not know why. Thankfully the storm looked far enough away that it would not disrupt her buggy ride with Jacob.

Esther smiled at the thought of Jacob. She could relax around him. Jacob always made her smile. She stared down the road, but he was not there. She strained her ears for the sound of his horse's hooves, but could not hear anything.

Esther was still worried Lizzie would come out and speak with her, maybe even scold her, so she wondered if she should walk down the road a little ways. Instead, she decided to walk into the garden and do some weeding. The urge to do household chores had gotten the better of her. She wasn't wearing gloves, so she would have to avoid the nettle, but she could place the weeds in a little pile on the ground and collect them later.

On her way to the herb garden, Esther stopped to smell the roses. She loved fragrant roses and was glad that they had medicinal purposes, being antiseptic and good for lowering cholesterol. Otherwise, her mother would have uprooted them long ago.

Esther's mother had a variety of medicinal herbs as well as culinary herbs and many, of course, suited both purposes. Esther's favorite herb was peppermint, as she loved meadow tea. Esther was also partial to rosemary. She bent down and untangled some weeds that were winding their way through the peppermint leaves.

Old Mrs. Graber had a large medicinal herb garden and had given the girls herbs to help them heal faster. Esther was sure her remedies had helped, and in fact, many of the people in the community went to Mrs. Graber for her remedies. When Esther and her sisters were children, Mrs. Graber had made tobacco salve to be rubbed on the chest and it had always made the flu run its course quickly. Esther pulled some weeds from the pokeroot and then moved on to the pennyroyal and burdock. They had no weeds, so she moved on to the comfrey.

Esther had just pulled a weed from the chamomile when she saw Jacob's buggy. She raced to open the little gate to the garden. Just as Jacob reined his horse to a stop, she called out, "Am I glad to see you!"

"Oh that's good. Changed your mind about me, have you?" Jacob asked with a wink.

"Get me out of here and I'll tell you all about it," Esther said, not minding for once that Jacob was teasing her.

When they were safely trotting away from the Millers' house, Esther let out a long sigh. "I was afraid my mother would forbid me to go on the buggy ride with you, and I also thought Lizzie Yoder might try to stop me."

"Now I'm really beginning to wonder," Jacob said. "Are we now dating for real?"

Esther laughed. "Of course not. It's just that I've had the most dreadful time. You do know that Lizzie Troyer is staying with us? She's staying in the *gross-mammi haus* with Mary."

"*Jah*, I had heard that," Jacob said. "Everyone knows."

"Lizzie doesn't seem to get on too well with poor Mary, and she obviously thinks Mary talks too much. And what's more, *Mamm* invited Lizzie to stay with us simply because she's Amos's sister."

"But I'm sure your parents would have invited one of the Troyers to stay," Jacob pointed out.

Esther shook her head. "*Nee*, I mean *jah*, but what I mean is that *Mamm* particularly chose Lizzie so she could invite Amos over more often. In fact, Amos came to dinner last night. Did you know that?"

"No, I didn't know that."

There was definitely tension in Jacob's voice and Esther was glad she had such a good friend who would be concerned that her mother was trying to force her onto Amos when she didn't want to marry him.

"So your mother is still trying to encourage you to marry Amos, is she?" Jacob asked tersely.

"She sure is," Esther said. "In fact, she's stepped up her efforts. And now I've got Lizzie at me too, so it's Lizzie and *Mamm* both trying to encourage me to marry Amos."

"Has Lizzie actually said something to you?" Jacob asked her.

Esther made a snorting sound. "Yes, she said quite a lot of things to me about it."

"Did you tell her you were going on a buggy ride with me?" Jacob asked.

"Of course I did," Esther said. "I kept going on and on about it but they just kept going on and on about Amos, how wonderful Amos is. I mean, he's nice and good-looking and all that..."

Jacob brought the horse to a halt and looked over at Esther. "So you think he's nice and good-looking?"

"Well, sure," Esther said, "but that's not the point. I don't feel any romantic spark with him and when I told *Mamm* and Lizzie that, they got angry."

Jacob raised his eyebrows. "They actually got angry?"

"They sure did."

"Why, they should be happy that you're marrying me," Jacob said with a chuckle. "I am a good man. I'm good-looking and a nice person too."

Esther playfully hit his arm. "Where are we going, Jacob?"

"You'll see. It was good no one was hurt when the house burned down," Jacob added thoughtfully. "I've been out there helping the other *menner*. An *Englischer* with some heavy machinery donated his time and cleared everything away, leaving a nice house site for when we start building."

"Yes, I heard that. It was very good of the *Englischer*," Esther said. "I felt sorry for Amos because his eyebrows were singed badly."

"So you saw Amos after the fire, did you?" Jacob asked her.

"Yes, I've already told you, haven't I?" Esther said. "He came for dinner last night."

"Oh yes, silly me. You did just tell me that," Jacob said easily, but Esther could hear the tension in his tone. "Did you invite him?"

"No, *Mamm* invited him. Why would I invite him, Jacob? You're not making any sense today."

Jacob did not respond, but simply said, "We're going down this lane."

"I should think that obvious, Jacob Hostetler," Esther said sternly. "You know, you really are quite strange today."

"I'm always strange," Jacob said with a laugh. "You'll have to get used to that when we're married."

Esther laughed at Jacob's joke.

"Is this a good place for a picnic by the pond?" he asked her.

"Are we having a picnic?" Esther said. "I thought we were only pretending to go on a buggy ride."

Jacob laughed. "We are pretending to have a picnic as well," he said. "Don't object, or all our pretend food will go to waste."

Esther laughed and hopped down from the buggy. It was such a relief to spend time with Jacob. She was always relaxed around him and there was never any tense silence like there was with Amos. Plus the Millers' house had also been a source of tension lately after Lizzie's arrival and with her mother set on her marrying Amos.

Jacob tied his horse, Barney, to a low branch, leaving him in the pleasant shade, and returned to their picnic spot on the grass. Esther smoothed down her simple dress, happy to watch as Jacob unpacked the basket. For their picnic by the pond, this time he had brought sandwiches and lemonade, grilled chicken, peppered deviled eggs, and cornbread salad.

Jacob spread a rug out on the grass and then opened a basket. Esther peered inside. "I'm a very good boyfriend, aren't I?" he said with a smirk.

Esther reached for the grilled chicken. "Yes, you're a very good pretend boyfriend."

"Well then, I'll take all the food away from you since you don't want to pretend to eat it," Jacob said, making a move to take the picnic basket.

"*Nee*!" Esther cried. "There's no reason for us not to eat this. It looks good. Surely you didn't prepare it yourself."

"I personally fetched it from my mother," he said with his crooked smile.

Esther laughed. It was a clear summer's day. The sunlight reflected on the pond, casting a silver glow upon the ripples caused by the ducks.

After Esther ate some grilled chicken, she said, "*Denki*, Jacob. *Denki* so much."

"What for?" he asked.

Esther waved her hands expansively. "For all this.

For helping me relax and for pretending to be my boyfriend."

"I'm happy to pretend to be your boyfriend, Esther," Jacob said. "That's what friends are for."

"I'm glad I have a friend as good as you," said Esther earnestly.

Jacob regarded her from underneath his long lashes. "Esther, you don't seem your usual self, if you don't mind me saying so. Normally you laugh more."

"You do know me well," Esther remarked. "Even my own sisters haven't noticed that I'm not my usual self."

"Why is that then, if I'm not prying?"

Esther sighed. "It's *Mamm*. She won't let up with her matchmaking, but I'm used to *Mamm* and her ways. Now that Lizzie has come, it's even harder."

"You said Lizzie is trying to encourage you to marry her *bruder*?"

Esther nodded. "Yes, it's that, and now that *Mamm* has someone who agrees with her, it's made her much worse. The two of them are at me all the time and I don't get any rest. It's really tiring. *Mamm* gets cross that I don't want to marry Amos, and she is not good to be around when she's in a bad mood."

"You really don't want to marry Amos?" Jacob asked.

Esther looked up into his face. "No, I've already told you that. Why do you keep asking me?"

"I thought you might secretly like him, but were having trouble admitting it to yourself because your mother wants you to marry him."

Esther chuckled. "*Nee,* Jacob, what an imagination you have! If I liked someone, I wouldn't really be concerned with what my mother thought." Her hand flew to her mouth. "Oh, that sounds bad, but you know what I mean."

"Yes, I always know what you mean, Esther," Jacob said. "I'm dismayed to see you so sad. In all the years I've known you, I've never seen you so sad."

"Well you make me happy, Jacob," Esther said. "You're the best pretend boyfriend a girl could ever have."

For some reason Jacob did not seem too pleased with the compliment, and Esther did not know why.

Esther lay in the summer sun. The soft breeze stirred the surface of the pond, while ducks raced here and there, through the rustling reeds.

"Thank you for going to so much trouble," said Esther, sleepily. "I could get used to picnics by the pond with you." The sun pressed upon her bare face, and it made her feel tired and content. The company helped her good mood too.

When Jacob had asked her to go on the buggy ride with him, she was a little hesitant at first, though it would help her with the Amos situation. Martha and Rebecca would tease her about falling in love with Jacob, of that she had no doubt. She had decided to go in the end, and now felt very happy with her choice.

Jacob handed her a cooling glass of lemonade. "No problem," he replied with a mischievous wink. "I hope Martha and Rebecca don't tease you too much."

"Sometimes I think that you can read my mind."

She watched Jacob eat his grilled chicken, fascinated by the freckles splattering his nose. In the summertime, all the Hostetler brothers were baked golden by their work with their father on the farm, so his freckles would often be camouflaged by the tan. Esther could not remember if she had ever sat this close to Jacob before. Perhaps the summer light drew out all these little curiosities about a person you could never see in the dimmer months.

"I wish I could," Jacob said, after a minute. He took a sip of his lemonade. "Then I wouldn't have to ask you so many questions."

"You want to ask me questions?" Esther replied, unable to keep the surprise out of her voice.

"Sure. Like, how come you agreed to a buggy ride with me today, when you know Martha and Rebecca are going to spend the next week teasing you endlessly? Surely Amos is not that bad?"

Amos isn't that bad, and some people are worth all the teasing in the world, thought Esther. "I don't mind the teasing," she said. "It's worth it for lemonade this good. I still can't believe how much trouble you went to. Even Barney seems to be enjoying himself."

"He's a good horse," replied Jacob, simply.

They watched as Barney lazily flicked away flies with the sweep of his tail. The ducks, curious about the pair sitting by their pond, waddled over to steal the crusts off the sandwiches. Esther laughed as the smallest, although the most courageous, duck nipped at the crumbs dropped by its larger friends. Jacob watched her while she laughed, and she could feel the blush creeping into her cheeks.

"Have you always had freckles?" she blurted out, desperate to break the quiet.

"Oh." Jacob hesitated. He was surprised, perhaps, by the randomness of her question. "Actually, I did not know I had freckles?"

"Millions of them."

"Oh, good," he replied, his crooked grin making Esther's heart flutter. She laughed too. "Girls like freckles?" He turned and gazed at Esther with a sudden intensity. "Girls do like freckles, don't they?"

"They would like your freckles," whispered Esther, placing a hand on her prayer *kapp* to make sure no curls had escaped. It also meant she could shade her face with the palm of her hand. She really was blushing now, and the intense gaze of Jacob was not helping. "I mean, all the girls love the Hostetler brothers, don't they?"

"You don't need *all* the girls to love you. Just the right one," said Jacob. He no longer smiled now. Esther wished he would. The sight of his signature grin made her melt.

"I appreciate you doing this for me," she volunteered. "I hate to be dishonest with our families and friends, but what else can I do when everyone wants me to marry Amos?"

"I'd do anything to stop you from marrying Amos. Wait. No. I only meant that I would do anything to help you avoid a marriage your heart was not in. That's all. I have nothing against Amos, even if he is good-looking." Jacob did smile now, though a little sheepishly. "Besides I get to spend a nice day with a beautiful girl. It's a win all around for me."

"You're not so bad yourself," Esther said.

Jacob swallowed hard. "It's none of my business, and it is probably a really silly question, but how come you're not interested in Amos? Is there—there is not someone else, is there?"

"No," Esther said, quickly. She took a sip of the lemonade while Jacob fixed his gaze upon her. "There's no spark with Amos, Jacob. I'm not interested in him at all, though I couldn't give you a solid reason why. I keep coming back to the lack of a connection. It isn't a reason I can tell my *familye* though. My *mudder* just doesn't understand such things as true love."

"Your mother really is set on you marrying Amos, isn't she?"

"She is. I don't know if this plan's even going to stop her matchmaking ways eventually. I wish it would. If I married Amos, I fear it would be a very unhappy marriage. I don't want to raise my children in an unhappy home."

"I can't wait to have *kinner*," replied Jacob, with a sigh.

Esther imagined Jacob with children. "You'd make a very good father," she said, placing the picnic things back in the basket. "I hope you find someone who will make a good *mudder* to your children."

"I think I already have," he replied, quietly, and Esther did not hear him.

Chapter Ten

As soon as Jacob drove away, Esther's good mood evaporated at once. Lizzie was standing on the front porch, her arms crossed. "They're all hard at work making pies for the fundraiser," she said in a scolding tone.

Esther felt horribly guilty. She had been away enjoying herself with Jacob while her sisters, Mary, and her mother had been working hard in the kitchen.

"I'll work extra hard to make up for it," Esther said, and she meant every word.

She hurried into the kitchen and was met with a black look from her mother. Esther had expected that.

"We've made so many pies," Mary said by way of greeting. "We've made pumpkin pies, lemon meringue pies, peanut butter pies, cream pies, blackberry pies, Dutch apple pies, chocolate cream pies, blueberry pies, peach pies, pecan pies, sugarless apple pies, coconut cream pies, rhubarb pies, black raspberry pies, and raspberry cream pies, strawberry rhubarb pies, cherry pies, and butterscotch cream pies." She stopped to draw breath.

Martha and Rebecca giggled, but Lizzie's face was bright red. "How can you remember so many pies!" she said angrily.

Mary's face fell as she turned back to her duties.

"Esther, you can make apple pies," her mother snapped, handing her a bowl of brown sugar. Esther did not notice what was in the bowl and asked, "Am I making the sugarless apple pies or the normal ones?"

Her mother held up her hands, palms upward, and rolled her eyes. "Esther, you need to concentrate. I have obviously set brown sugar in front of you. And here is the granulated sugar."

Esther at once poured the brown sugar and the granulated sugar along with flour, a small amount of cinnamon and nutmeg and a pinch of salt into a bowl and whisked it. She added butter and stirred until the mixture was crumbly. She did not want to look up at anyone because the tension in the room was so thick it could be cut with a knife. Esther then peeled the Macintosh apples. She placed the apples in the pie shell. She then beat eggs in a small bowl before adding cream and vanilla.

Mary was chatting away to Martha, but no one else was speaking. Esther didn't want to be scolded any longer. She felt bad for having such a good time with Jacob. Finally, Esther added sugar to the egg mixture and blended it, and then poured it over the apples.

"You made that very well," Lizzie said.

Esther looked up, surprised at the compliment.

"You will make some *mann* a good *fraa*," Lizzie added.

Esther forced a smile on her face and nodded. She knew only too well whose *fraa* Lizzie wanted her to be and it was Amos. Her heart sank. She had just returned from a buggy ride with Jacob. She had expected Lizzie and her mother to be upset about that, but she certainly hadn't expected them to continue to encourage her to marry Amos.

Esther resumed peeling apples, while Mary and her sisters chatted happily. Lizzie and Mrs. Miller spoke in low tones. Mrs. Miller kept insisting that Lizzie shouldn't help, so Lizzie sat on a wooden chair and spoke with Mrs. Miller.

"How many pies are we making, Mrs. Miller?" Mary asked. "Not that I'm complaining, of course. These pies will be such a help to the Troyer family and you, of course, Lizzie."

Lizzie merely scowled at her.

"What's your favorite pie, Martha?" Mary said. "My favorite is lemon meringue pie or maybe cherry pie. No, I think it's butterscotch cream pie." She patted her stomach. "I like all sorts of pies."

"That's obvious," Lizzie muttered.

Esther was shocked. She threw herself into making more pies in the hopes of raising more money for the fundraiser so Lizzie could leave their house all the sooner.

"My favorite is chocolate cream pie, of course," Martha said.

Lizzie turned her attention to Martha. “Why do you say ‘of course’, Martha?”

“Because I’m going to be a chocolate maker,” Martha said.

Mrs. Miller rolled her eyes.

“A chocolate maker?” Lizzie repeated in shock.

“Yes, when I go on *rumspringa* I’m going to make chocolates and sell them,” Martha said happily. “Did you go on *rumspringa*, Lizzie?”

“I most certainly did not,” Lizzie said. “I found I had no interest in following the ways of the *Englisch*, even for a short time. Hannah didn’t go on *rumspringa* did she, Rachel?”

Mrs. Miller shook her head. “*Nee*, and nor did Esther. Martha will be my first *dochder* to go on *rumspringa*.”

Martha beamed while Lizzie looked aghast.

Esther just wanted to run out into the fields. Maybe Lizzie would get tired of staying with them and stay with someone else. She knew *Gott* worked in mysterious ways, and maybe He had plans for Lizzie, plans that did not include staying at the Millers’ house for much longer. She smiled to herself.

“What are you smiling at, Esther?” Lizzie asked her, as if it were a crime to smile.

“I just had a happy thought,” Esther said, peeling apples furiously.

“I bet it was about Jacob,” Mary said. “You haven’t told us about your buggy ride, Esther. Did you have a nice time in your buggy ride with Jacob?”

Martha and Rebecca poked each other in the ribs and giggled.

"I had a lovely time, in fact. We had a picnic by the pond." Esther realized her tone was defiant, but by this point she didn't really care. She hadn't done anything wrong and it was stressful the way her mother and Lizzie were treating her. "We had grilled chicken, peppered deviled eggs, and cornbread salad."

"Where would Jacob get that food?" Lizzie said.

"Clearly, his mother gave it to him," Mrs. Miller said. "She obviously approves."

Lizzie pouted so hard that her mouth puckered. Esther wondered if she would get permanent wrinkles.

"Well, a buggy ride doesn't always mean marriage, thankfully," Lizzie said to Mrs. Miller.

Esther was annoyed they were discussing her when she was right there, but there was nothing she could do about it.

"Did you go fishing?" Mary asked.

"*Nee*," Esther said. "We just went for a buggy ride and had a picnic by the pond."

"How romantic," Mary said wistfully. "I wish a *mann* would take me on a buggy ride and for a picnic by the pond. We could have strawberry pudding and all sorts of pies as well as what you had, Esther. Did you say grilled chicken, deviled eggs, and cornbread salad?"

"*Jah*," Esther said with a smile. "I'm sure you will be asked on a buggy ride one day, Mary."

Martha and Rebecca agreed. Much to Esther's surprise, Mrs. Miller did too. "You would make a man a good *fraa*, Mary. You have a lovely nature. You're kind-hearted and a very hard worker."

Mary's jaw fell open and Esther realized her own jaw was open as well. Lizzie likewise looked surprised at Mrs. Miller's praise for Mary. Esther realized her mother had grown quite fond of Mary and wondered if this was her mother's way of signaling to Lizzie not to be mean to Mary any longer. She thought that might be the case when Lizzie shifted uncomfortably in her seat.

"What time is the fundraiser tomorrow?" Esther asked her mother.

"I should hope you would know that, Esther," her mother said in a sarcastic tone. "After all, surely you saw signs while on your buggy ride, didn't you?"

"Yes I did, *Mamm*," Esther said meekly.

Esther's mother banged a pot, startling Esther. "Then you should have noticed the time it started," she said angrily.

"It starts at ten," Mary told her.

"You were obviously too taken with Jacob to read the signs," Rebecca said with a giggle.

Esther was upset. Mrs. Miller was furious now and she would be even more furious at the fundraiser.

And Esther was right. The day of the fundraiser was bright and sunny, but it had been an unpleasant morning. Mrs. Miller had banged pots and pans around constantly and snapped at everyone who spoke to her, apart from Lizzie. Esther lamented the fact that the fundraiser was to be held at the Hostetlers'. Her mother was icy to Mrs. Hostetler at the best of times, and Esther couldn't see this would end well.

Her mother's bad mood continued on the buggy ride to the Hostetlers' house. "It's silly to have the fundraiser so soon," Mrs. Miller grumbled to Mr. Miller.

"Rachel, they need money. I am sure Lizzie's *familye* will be grateful for the money coming so soon. Everyone is organizing the big auction fundraiser, but that will take more time. This will bring in immediate money."

Mrs. Miller made a strangled sound at the back of her throat.

"It's a good idea to have this pie fundraiser so soon, isn't it, Lizzie?"

"Yes, Abraham," Lizzie said after hesitating. Her voice held no enthusiasm, and Esther wondered if she was agreeing to be polite, while not wanting to disagree overtly with Mrs. Miller.

As the buggy approached the Hostetlers' farm, Esther was surprised to see a field full of buggies as well as scooters, and also several vans that had driven people from other Amish communities there.

Jacob was standing on the road directing traffic. "*Hiya*, Jacob," Mr. Miller called. Esther noticed he elbowed his wife ever so slightly. "*Hullo*," she said, although there was no warmth in her voice.

Lizzie at least greeted him more warmly. "*Denki* to you and your parents for holding the fundraiser here," she said, and Esther realized her tone was genuine.

Mary piped up. "Imagine! Look at all these people! I've never seen so many people in one spot before. They're everywhere! Why, it's just amazing how many people there are, and all in the one place too. I haven't seen so many people even at a big meeting or a wedding. I haven't seen so many people in the one spot. Look at those people over there—there are so many of them. How can you manage to tell them where to go, Jacob?" she asked.

Jacob responded with a chuckle, but Mr. Miller was already driving the buggy to the appointed place.

Earlier that morning, Mr. Miller and Mary had driven all the pies to the Hostetlers'. Mrs. Miller had refused to allow Esther to go, presumably because she wanted to keep her away from Jacob. That upset Esther, but again there was nothing Esther could do about it.

Mary was still talking. "Wow, it's a parking lot! This whole huge front field here at the Hostetlers' farm is a buggy parking lot! I've never seen so many buggies in the one place. Look at all the different types of buggies here. I've never seen so many."

Martha and Rebecca giggled. Esther noted the expression on Lizzie's face. Her cheeks grew redder and redder, but clearly, Lizzie dared not reprimand Mary again in front of Mrs. Miller.

"Yes, so you haven't seen so many in your community?" Mrs. Miller asked Mary.

"*Nee*, *nee*, *nee*!" Mary said in an excitable manner. "What are we going to do to help today?" she asked Mrs. Miller.

"We're going to sell the pies," Mrs. Miller said.

"Unless of course Mrs. Hostetler has something else in mind." She frowned deeply as she spoke.

Mr. Miller told everyone to get out of the buggy and said he would see to the horse. Mrs. Miller led Lizzie and the girls to a huge tent. "I assume this is the pie tent," she said, and was about to say more when Hannah appeared. "Hannah!" Mrs. Miller said with delight. "You haven't been to visit much lately."

"I just know that you're busy," Hannah said absently. "I'm working at the salad bar today, and you're all selling the pies?"

"Yes, we are all selling the pies," Mrs. Miller said.

Esther walked over to the salad bar in the middle of the tent. Bowls of salad ingredients sat on wooden boxes. "Katie Hostetler and I prepared the salad ingredients," Hannah told them.

Mary peered at the ingredients. "Oh wow, look at all that food! I can see bacon and ham. Oh, and there's egg salad and all the shredded carrots, cauliflower, cucumbers, and celery!"

"I would rather be on the dessert table," Hannah said with a laugh. "Still, I've lost my appetite for sweet things lately. When I was preparing the bacon yesterday, I felt a little sick."

Mrs. Miller reached out to feel Hannah's forehead. "I hope you're not coming down with a fever."

Hannah waved her concerns away. "*Nee,* I'm fine, I'm sure."

"Can we see the dessert tent, please?" Mary said. Without waiting for a response, she hurried over to the dessert tent. Mrs. Hostetler appeared at the tent and looked shocked to see Mrs. Miller. Mrs. Miller looked even more shocked. "*Hullo*, Katie," Mrs. Miller said tersely.

"*Hullo*, Rachel." Mrs. Hostetler's greeting was far warmer.

Lizzie hurried over to Katie and gushed. "It is so kind of you to hold the pie fundraiser here, Katie," she said, seemingly not caring what Mrs. Miller thought for once.

"Yes, it's very good of you," Mrs. Miller said. "Now where has Mary got to?"

"She's in the dessert tent," Esther told her.

"Well, we'll find her and take her to the pie tent," Mrs. Miller said. She nodded goodbye to Katie Hostetler.

"Look at all these tea bottles and bottles of water in ice!" Mary said excitedly. "But can you believe the dessert table! I've never seen so many desserts in the one place. Look at all those whoopie pies. These ones have peanut butter fillings and those ones are chocolate. I don't know what the white filling is, but it sure looks good. And you could have ice cream with it." Mary was trembling with excitement.

When they reached the pie tent, Esther gasped at the number of pies. She thought her family had made a huge amount of pies, but that amount was eclipsed by the number of pies on offer.

"How much do we charge for the pies?" Esther asked.

"Esther, sometimes I worry about you," her mother said. "You have become less focused and observant of late. You have been off in your own world and have become a dreamer. That is not *gut*, not *gut* at all. Can't you see all these wooden boxes around? What do you think they are for? Have you not noticed the word 'donation' is clearly marked on them?"

Esther felt foolish. "I see," she said. "Is everything for sale by donation?"

"*Jah*, and I believe that was discussed at the table several times today and yesterday," her mother said. "Was your mind somewhere else?"

"It most likely was," Esther said, at first not realizing the implications of her mother's words. Her mother was regarding her with narrowed eyes and it was clear her mother thought she was thinking about Jacob.

Esther had thought she would be bored, but the morning passed quickly. Many *Englischers* also attended and she noticed they made sizeable donations.

"Isn't it good when the whole community comes together," Mary said in between serving customers. "*Englischers* coming together with us for this good cause. Isn't it *wunderbar*!"

"Yes, it certainly is," Esther said. "And I think quite a bit of money has been raised as well."

An *Englisch* lady stopped at the table. "Do you have anything that's sugar free?" she asked Esther. "My husband is a diabetic."

"Yes, come over here," Esther said. She took the lady to a large pile of sugar free apple pies.

"These would freeze, wouldn't they?" the lady asked her.

Esther nodded. "Yes, they do freeze well."

"I'll have five," the lady said.

Esther put them all in a box for the lady. "I'll have someone carry them for you, or would you like to leave them here until you're ready to go?"

"I'm about to leave now, but I can carry them myself," the lady said. "So you're raising money because the house was destroyed by fire?"

"That's right," Esther said. "No one was hurt, though."

The woman nodded. "And wasn't the house insured? Is that why you're raising money?"

"No, we don't insure our houses," Esther told her.

The lady gasped and clutched her throat. "You don't insure anything? Why?"

Esther shook her head. "Purchasing insurance shows lack of faith in *Gott's* provision. If anyone needs money, then the community rallies around to help them," Esther said.

"That's so nice. What a lovely thing to do for your neighbors." The woman took a large wad of bills from her wallet and pushed them all into the donation box. Esther had not seen such a large sum of money and did her best not to gasp. She sucked in her cheeks so as not to look overly surprised. "Thank you," she said to the lady.

The lady gave a little wave and walked away with the box of pies.

Esther's heart sang. So many people were donating, and if other *Englischers* made donations of this sort, it would go a long way toward helping the

Troyers. And Esther knew that the auction fundraiser would bring in even more money. She was relieved on behalf of the Troyers.

"Esther, you, Mary, Rebecca, and Martha can take a break now but not for long, mind you. Go to the buggy and fetch the sandwiches."

"Would you like some sandwiches, *Mamm*?" Esther asked her.

"*Nee.* When you come back I will go away for a few minutes, but for now you girls go and have lunch. The food is in the back of the buggy."

Mary rubbed her stomach. "I'm starving, I can tell you! Being around all this food and not being able to eat it is so hard. I've never had to exercise so much willpower in my whole life." She laughed and the others laughed with her.

Jacob was still directing traffic and Esther was surprised to see people still arriving, although nowhere near as many as there had been that morning. There was someone speaking with Jacob, but she couldn't see who it was from a distance. When they got closer, she saw it was Jessie Yoder.

"*Hiya*, Jacob," Mary called out, much to Esther's dismay. She wanted to slip behind them, unnoticed.

Jacob spun around. His cheeks were flushed red. Why did he look so guilty? And why did Jessie look so triumphant?

Esther's stomach clenched.

Chapter Eleven

Church meetings were held every other week. As Esther sat on one of the hard, backless, wooden benches in the Grabers' *haus*, she noted from time to time that Jacob was leaning forward and trying to catch her eye. She knew him well enough to realize that it was his way of signaling that he wanted to speak to her later, so when she stood up after kneeling for one of the long prayers, she nodded imperceptibly at him.

Esther's mind floated away to when she and Jacob were children, and had first gone skating on the pond together. She had been a little afraid at first, but then Jacob had taken her hand, and at once, all was right with the world. Esther had no idea why that memory had popped unbidden into her mind, for it was summer now, and many years later. She supposed that she had remembered the connection that she and Jacob had always had.

The minister was preaching on moving forward, on not looking back to the past. "Brethren, I count not myself to have apprehended: but this one thing I do, forgetting those things which are behind, and reaching forth unto those things which are before. I press toward the mark for the prize of the high calling of God in Christ Jesus," he quoted. The minister went on to explain that everyone should do everything that they can to keep moving forward in *Gott's* plan, rather than in their own plan.

I hope Mamm's paying attention to the preaching, Esther thought, a little unkindly, *and then she'll leave it to* Gott *to matchmake instead.*

The day grew hotter and more humid, and Esther was glad when the long service was over. She had nearly fallen asleep during the typically tremendously slow singing followed by the lengthy preaching.

While the *haus* was cleared so that the benches could be converted to tables for eating, Esther walked outside to look for Jacob. She figured she didn't have long, as soon everyone would be ushered back for the meal, and the young men and women usually ate in separate shifts.

To her dismay, Esther saw that Linda Graber had Jacob cornered near a tree by a horse pasture, and was talking to him in an animated fashion. Esther wandered over, trying to look casual. She swatted some flies away and screwed up her nose at the smell of horse manure. Esther loved the smell of horses, but the fresh manure on a hot day was not her favorite fragrance, especially as it attracted the annoying, buzzing flies.

Jacob looked up with some relief when he caught Esther's eye. "*Hiya*, Esther!"

"*Hiya*!" Esther returned his greeting. Linda turned around and it was clear to Esther that Linda wasn't too happy to see her.

Linda didn't leave, so the three of them stood around awkwardly. Finally, Linda broke the silence. "It's the Singing tonight," she said, stating the obvious.

Jacob and Esther nodded. Jacob frowned at Esther as if to say, *I need to talk with you.*

Esther raised her eyebrows at him, as if to reply, *What can I do about it?*

Linda continued, shooting a sidelong glance at Esther. "You're going to the Singing, aren't you, Jacob?"

"*Jah*." Jacob looked at his feet, and another awkward silence ensued.

Finally, Esther decided to take matters into her own hands. Time was running out and soon the women would be called inside to eat. "Jacob's driving me home after the Singing tonight."

Linda gasped, and hurried away. Esther at once felt bad. "Sorry I told Linda that you were taking me home after the Singing, Jacob. Is that all right? I just thought of it on the spur of the moment. Or did you want to take Linda home after the Singing?"

"*Nee*, Esther, don't be silly. We're supposed to be dating, or have you forgotten already? Did you forget the buggy ride? Anyway, that's what I wanted to talk with you about. I was actually going to suggest that I drive you home after the Singing, so that word will get out that we're dating."

Esther swiped at a fly a few times until she realized it was a bee. "So you don't mind that I said that then?" When Jacob shook his head and smiled at her, she continued. "Are you certain you don't like Linda though? She sure was upset when you said you were taking me home."

"Jealous?" Jacob's eyes twinkled.

"*As if*, Jacob Hostetler," Esther snapped. "*As if.* I'm being considerate, that's all. I don't want my own plans to ruin your future plans for a *fraa*."

"You don't have to explain yourself to me, Esther," Jacob said in an amused voice. "If you say you're not jealous, then I'll believe you."

"*Hmmpf*," Esther snorted. "You're the most infuriating *mann*."

Esther went to strut off, but Jacob caught her by the arm. "You'd better think something up next time instead of leaving it all to me."

"What do you mean?"

"I came up with the idea of driving you home from the Singing—well, you also thought of it, but I was about to suggest it. It's what courting couples do. You know, your *mudder's* no fool. She knows you don't like Amos and she could easily suspect that our dating is actually fake."

Esther rubbed her chin. "*Jah*, *gut* point. I actually hadn't thought it through."

At that moment, the women were called inside to

eat. As Esther made to leave, she said, "I'll have to think up what else to do."

"It's easy," Jacob said in a low tone, as Esther's *schweschders* were heading over to her. "Just think what dating couples usually do. How about I take you on another buggy ride soon? That'll put a stop to anyone's suspicions."

"*Jah*!" Esther exclaimed. "That's brilliant, Jacob. *Denki* so much for all your help with this." Esther thought it over some more. "The only thing is, Martha and Rebecca have been teasing me relentlessly after our buggy ride. I'm not sure another one's such a *gut* idea after all."

Jacob shrugged. "It's what dating couples do. What would you prefer, teasing, or your *mudder* pushing you and Amos together?"

Martha and Rebecca had reached them, so Esther simply said, "*Jah*, you're right," before leaving Jacob to go inside the *haus* with Martha and Rebecca. She felt blessed that she had such a *gut* friend as Jacob, who was putting quite some effort into helping her pretend that the two of them were dating.

Esther took her seat at the table in the room for the young women, flanked by Martha and Rebecca. "Why didn't you tell us?" Martha hissed.

Esther reached for the *kaffi* pot. "What do you mean?"

"Don't play innocent with us," Rebecca said in a low tone. "We overheard what you said to *Datt* and *Mamm* last week. You told us you were going on a buggy ride with Jacob and you made out to us that it didn't mean anything. We were waiting for you to tell us that you really liked him, but you didn't." Her voice rose in indignation.

Esther poured herself a mug of *kaffi*. "You two tease me too much," she said, hoping she wouldn't have to lie to her *schweschders*.

"We knew anyway," Martha said.

"You did?" Esther was puzzled.

"*Jah*, we knew Jacob and you liked each other. Everyone knows!"

Esther raised her eyebrows. "They do?"

Esther made to take some bread but Rebecca moved the plate away from her. "Stop answering our questions with questions. We know all about how much you like Jacob, so there's nothing more to be said. You didn't even admit it after the buggy ride. We just wish you'd told us, that's all."

"I'm sorry I didn't tell you both, truly. Now, Rebecca, eat some bread before you eat any *schnitz* pie."

Rebecca rolled her eyes. "If I had *der Bo,* I'd tell you about it. It's not fair."

"I'd tell you too," Martha said, "but my boyfriend will be *Englisch*. Wait and see!"

Esther put her hands over her ears. "My whole *familye's ferhoodled*," she said to no one in particular.

Her sisters didn't appear to be offended at being called crazy, and just tucked into the apple butter, bread, cheese, pickles, *schnitz* pies, and *Church spread* of marshmallows and peanut butter.

As Esther put some cheese onto her bread to make a sandwich, she felt eyes upon her. She looked up into the face of Jessie Yoder who had just arrived and taken a seat opposite her. Esther smiled automatically, but Jessie looked away, although not before she had fixed Esther with a withering glare.

Esther remembered then that Hannah had told her some time ago that Jessie had a crush on Jacob. *I hope I haven't put my foot in it*, she thought. *I must ask Jacob how he feels about Jessie. It seems obvious to me how Jessie feels about Jacob.*

Jacob smiled to himself as he watched Esther walk away with her younger *schweschders*. Esther had suggested that he drive her home after the Singing later that night. Jacob wanted to jump up and down and scream with joy, even though on Esther's part, it was all pretense. Esther had held Jacob's heart for as long as he could remember, and he had always wanted to marry her.

Esther had even seemed jealous, but Jacob didn't want to get his hopes up. Still, today had gone well.

Jacob looked out at the horizon of rolling hills and trees. There was quite a wind today, and Jacob watched absently as it picked up leaves and spun them around. He looked up, and saw Jessie Yoder watching him from a window. He didn't know why, but a shiver ran up his spine.

Chapter Twelve

The songs at the night Singings were never sung as slowly as the hymns in the church meetings. The church meetings always used the *Ausbund* as their only hymn book, but at the night Singings, *Heartland Hymns* was the most used hymnal. Esther was strangely looking forward to tonight's Singing, although she couldn't really figure out why.

Esther and her sisters often spent time socializing and fellowshipping with the other younger members of the community after the morning church meeting, but today, her *mudder* wanted all three girls at home.

As Esther left in the *familye* buggy driven by her *daed*, she looked back wistfully at the youth enjoying themselves. Jacob caught her eye—he was talking to Jessie Yoder. The two of them were by themselves, several yards from the others. Esther felt a small pang of unease.

Later that night, Esther was heartily singing *In the Rifted Rock I'm Resting*, one of the gospel songs in *Heartland Hymns*, when she saw Jacob looking at her. She smiled back, and a warm, fuzzy feeling enveloped her.

As Esther sang the chorus, she thought about Jesus.

Now I'm resting, sweetly resting,
In the cleft once made for me;
Jesus, blessed Rock of Ages,
I will hide myself in Thee.

She thought how *Gott* loved the world so much that he gave His only Son Jesus to die on the cross for our sins. She thought how we are reconciled to *Gott* through faith in the precious blood of Jesus.

As Esther sang the last verse, her thoughts turned to Jacob.

In the rifted rock I'll hide me,
Till the storms of life are past;
All secure in this blest refuge,
Heeding not the fiercest blast.

Esther considered that *Gott* had truly blessed her with a friend such as Jacob. Jacob had always been her refuge, someone she had always gone to when she was troubled by anything, from the time she was a little child.

The heat of the gas lamps gradually raised the temperature of the humid summer night, and Esther's throat became dry from singing. When the community water cup was passed around, Esther took a deep gulp.

The Singing finished around ten o'clock, and most people headed for the tables, not to eat, but to drink the water, which was freely provided along with *kaffi*.

Esther was so intent on relieving her parched throat that she didn't hear Amos walk up beside her.

"*Hiya*, Esther."

"*Ach, hullo*," Esther said, with some surprise.

Amos fidgeted on the spot. "Esther, would I be able to drive you home tonight?"

Esther caught her breath. This was a disaster. Driving a girl home from a Singing was generally the first step in dating. "*Nee*, sorry, Amos, but Jacob's driving me home." Esther searched Amos's face for signs of disappointment, but to her surprise, he showed none. In fact, Esther even thought she could detect some relief. *Perhaps his* mudder's *trying matchmaking too, against his will*, Esther thought, pleased that she hadn't hurt Amos's feelings.

Esther looked at her younger sisters, Martha and Rebecca, and saw that they were eating and standing with each other. She cast her glance wider and saw that Jacob was talking to Jessie Yoder. They were standing close to each other, like they had been at the pie fundraiser.

Her stomach immediately knotted and her heart thumped loudly. *If Jacob wanted to date Jessie, he should've come straight out and told me*, she thought. Esther wondered why she was so upset, but figured that it was due to the fact that she did not want her *mudder* to keep up her matchmaking efforts and try to force her onto Amos Troyer, who, from all appearances, was just as unwilling as she was.

Jacob looked up and saw Esther's eyes on him. He

said something to Jessie and walked over to Esther, leaving Jessie scowling after him.

"Jacob, if you want to date Jessie, please don't let me stop you," she whispered. "I'd feel bad if you missed out on dating Jessie just to help me out."

"*Nee*, I think Jessie has a little crush on me," Jacob whispered back.

Esther nodded. "It seems to have been going on a long time."

Jacob smiled his crooked smile, which made Esther's heart beat widely, although she had no idea why. "I can't help it if girls find me irresistible."

"Jacob!" Esther exclaimed. "Don't be so prideful. *Eegeloob schtinkt.*" *Self-praise stinks.*

Jacob chuckled. "So you're not denying that I'm irresistible?"

Esther rolled her eyes and gave his arm a playful swipe.

Jacob ducked out of the way. "Anyway, do you want me to drive you home now, or do you want to stay around and eat first?"

Esther caught a glimpse of Jessie's narrowed eyes. "Let's go. We can eat something at my *haus*."

Jacob raised his eyebrows. "So, we're carrying it as far as that, are we? Eating at your *haus*?"

"*Jah*," Esther hissed, "of course. *Mamm's* the main person we have to fool, so we have to do what a dating couple would normally do, or she'll be suspicious. Well, only if it's okay with you, of course," she added.

"Of course I don't mind. No point in taking half measures." He looked quite pleased with himself.

Esther stared at Jacob. There was something behind his tone, but she couldn't quite put her finger on it.

"Why are you staring at me?"

Esther put her finger to her chin. "You're up to something, aren't you?"

"Who me?" Jacob put both his hands in the air and then chuckled. "Anyway, come along, *Mei Lieb*, I had better be driving you home."

When Jacob called Esther *My Love*, her stomach twisted into one big knot and her heart fluttered. She knew that Jacob was only saying that to keep up appearances, but the thought of a handsome *mann* calling her *My Love* made her tremble delightfully, even if that *mann* was only Jacob.

As Esther sat next to Jacob in his open-topped courting buggy, a thought occurred to her. "Jacob, why have you never taken a girl home after Singing?"

Jacob looked over at her and smiled. "Well, I am now."

Esther rolled her eyes again. Jacob always had that effect on her. "You know what I mean."

Jacob just shrugged and kept driving.

"I see you're dressed in your *for-gut* clothes," Esther continued. She looked at Jacob, his strong hands holding the reins, his kind face with its strong jaw, and his better-than-usual clothes.

"*Jah*, I can't go courting in my farming clothes."

Esther giggled.

"Do you think your *mudder* will be awake and sitting up, ready to scare me away?"

Jacob's tone was lighthearted, but Esther gritted her teeth. "Perhaps. My *schweschders* and I missed the volleyball before the Singing. I suspect *Mamm* took us home after the church meeting to keep me away from you."

Jacob navigated a sharp bend in the road before he spoke. "Your *vadder* approves of me, though?"

Esther hurried to reassure him. "Of course he does, Jacob, and your *bruder* works for him, and what's more, Noah's married to my *schweschder*. *Mamm's* fine about that now, so she'll come around to you in time." As soon as she'd said the words, Esther realized that she was acting as if dating Jacob was for real rather than pretend, and then laughed so hard she clutched her stomach.

"What's so funny?" Jacob turned to her, and although it was too dark to see his face, Esther could feel his eyes on her.

"For a minute I thought we were dating for real." Esther burst into a fit of giggles. When Jacob didn't respond, her mood grew more solemn. Menner, she thought, *there's just no understanding them. He appears to be offended that I was laughing about dating him, yet he knows it's all pretend. How strange.*

The two continued their journey in silence. The dark enveloped them, and Esther thought back to when she was a child, and afraid of the clothes hanging on the pegs on the wall. Her *mudder* had to tell her that the frightening shapes were just clothes and nothing sinister. Her *mudder* always scolded her for having an overactive imagination. Now, as they drove along, the tree branches seemed to reach out to clasp at her. Nevertheless, she felt safe with Jacob there. He would never let anything happen to her. He was strong, and gentle, and kind. When he did marry, his *fraa* would be a very blessed woman indeed. Esther was unable to suppress a little shudder.

As Jacob stopped the buggy outside Esther's *haus*, Mr. Miller came over to them. "I expect you'll be here for an hour to two, Jacob. I'll put your horse in a stall and give him some hay. You two young ones go ahead into the *haus*."

"*Denki*, Mr. Miller."

As the hour was late, Esther had hoped her parents and *schweschders* would be asleep, so that Jacob and she wouldn't have the stress of keeping up appearances. Sadly, that was not to be. Her *mudder* was sitting at the kitchen table, a tight-lipped smile on her face. "*Hullo*, Jacob."

"*Hullo*, Mrs. Miller."

Mrs. Miller nodded curtly to Jacob and then looked at Esther. "Did you have a *gut* time at the Singing, Esther?"

"*Jah*, *Mamm*, *denki*."

"*Gut*!" Mrs. Miller said the word almost as an accusation.

Jacob and Esther sat at the kitchen table, and the three of them sat in uncomfortable silence. After what seemed an age, Mr. Miller returned. He walked into the kitchen and then made a show of stretching and yawning. "*Ach*, I'm so tired. Aren't you tired, Rachel?"

Mrs. Miller glared at him. "*Nee*."

"Of course you are, Rachel. Let's go and get some sleep. *Guten nacht*, Jacob, Esther."

Jacob and Esther both said good night, and Mrs. Miller very reluctantly followed her husband out of the door and up the stairs.

When they were safely out of earshot, Esther laughed. "*Datt* made that obvious. Just as well we weren't dating. That would've been embarrassing."

Jacob laughed. "*Jah*." He rubbed his stomach. "Did you mention food? I'm starving, since you wouldn't let me eat at the Singing."

Esther let out a mock groan. "Sure, I'll make you a mug of hot chocolate. Now we have Shoo-fly pies, and rhubarb pie—oh, and there's Apple Pandowdy, but it's not hot. I could heat it."

"Do you have cream and nutmeg?"

"*Jah*."

"I prefer Apple Pandowdy cold, with cream and nutmeg, if that's okay. *Denki*," he added.

Esther went to make the hot chocolate, but then looked over her shoulder. "Oh, would you rather have corn soup with rivels? It would only take me about fifteen minutes to make it."

Jacob shook his head. "*Nee, denki*. I have a sweet tooth, which you'd better take notice of if you're going to make me a suitable *fraa*."

"*Hmmpf*!" Esther said, and threw an oven mitt at him. He caught it with one hand, and smiled triumphantly.

Jacob sat alone as Esther went to make him a mug of hot chocolate. He was a little embarrassed that he had called her *Mei Lieb*, My Love, earlier, but Esther clearly thought that was simply part of their pretense. He'd have to watch his words more closely from now on. Still, it was easy to forget that they were only *pretending* to be dating.

Esther returned with two hot chocolates and a plate of pumpkin whoopie pies.

"You like your *menner* plump, do you Esther? You're always trying to fatten me up."

Esther laughed. Jacob loved looking at Esther's face when she laughed. Her whole face lighted up, her blue eyes shone, and tiny little creases formed around her eyes.

"Your *mudder* wasn't happy to see me, as we predicted," he said. "I hope she has no objection to us getting married." Jacob carefully studied Esther's face for her reaction. So far, she appeared quite puzzled.

Esther leaned over to Jacob and whispered, "Do you think she's listening from the other room?"

Jacob just winked at her.

Chapter Thirteen

Mrs. Miller banged a saucepan. "Amos is coming to dinner tonight," she announced.

"Again? But he was just here the other day." Esther screwed up her nose at her *mudder.* "Why does he have to come again?" She knew she sounded whiny and rude, but she just did not care. It was simply intolerable that her *mudder* would continue with her matchmaking attempts when she clearly knew that she had gone on a buggy ride with Jacob.

Mrs. Miller stomped her foot and her eyes blazed. "Mind your manners, Esther. I shall invite anyone I choose to share our table. Amos is here to see Lizzie, of course."

Esther walked away from her *mudder* shaking her head. Sometimes it was no use arguing with her. Her *mudder* never really listened to her and besides, she could never see anyone's point of view but her own.

"Mind you, I'll need some help with the cooking."

Esther heard her *mudder's* comment as she walked

away. "*Jah, Mamm.*" It was obvious that her *mudder* was going to credit Esther with the cooking once more in an effort to impress Amos. That was a ploy that was too obvious to bother complaining about. Her *mudder* would just brush her words aside, even if she attempted to protest.

"And Esther, put on a clean dress for dinner, and clean yourself up a little." Her *mudder's* voice echoed through the *haus*.

"*Jah, Mamm,*" Esther called in reply, yet she had no intention of going to any trouble whatsoever for Amos or for anyone else who her *mudder* might invite to dinner.

Once Esther was in her room, she pulled off the dress she had been in all day and pulled on a fresh one. That was the least she would do to keep her *mudder* happy with her. She knew if she went down in the same dress, her *mudder* would only send her back to get changed. Esther sighed. *Why can't* Mamm *let me choose my own* mann*?* she thought. Esther did not even want to court anyone, but if she did, she was certain that she would not want anyone's help. Things like that just happen—she was certain of that.

Esther had only been in her room a few short moments before her *mudder* called for her again. "I'm coming, *Mamm,*" she called.

Esther hurried into the kitchen and pulled on a large apron that was used for cooking, a different one from those used for daywear. "What would you like me to do?"

Her *mudder* turned around with a wooden spoon

held in the air and ran her eyes up and down Esther, clearly not happy with what she saw. "Did you wash?"

"*Jah.*" Esther's eyes dropped to the floor. She had just lied to her *mudder*, but she could not go to a lot of fuss to wash before dinner. Esther always washed just before bedtime and she was not going to have a double washing just because her *mudder* was trying to push her onto a *mann* who was totally unsuited to her.

"*Gut*, and that dress is a *gut* color for you." Her *mudder* turned back to the saucepan in front of her, obviously forgetting Esther's question about what she wanted her to do.

Esther pulled out one of the chairs in the kitchen and slumped into it. She knew that her *mudder* liked to be the only one to do all the cooking on special occasions. Esther knew she would only be doing a tiny bit here and there to make it appear that she had cooked.

"You can shell the peas for me." Her *mudder* pointed to the green pods in the sink.

"*Jah, Mamm.*" Esther tried to make her tone as even as possible, as she knew that her *mudder* would take exception to her tone, no matter how even it was.

"What's wrong with you, Esther? Don't you know all the trouble I'm going to for you?"

Esther sighed. Her *mudder* was clearly in one of her moods. "I just said—*jah, Mamm.*"

Her mother slammed her wooden spoon down. "It was the way you said it. Sometimes I don't know why I bother."

There was nothing Esther could say, so she thought it best to stay silent and let her *mudder* have her say.

Mrs. Miller's face grew redder and redder. "I just want you to make a *gut* marriage and Amos is such a lovely boy."

Esther toyed with the idea of telling her *mudder* that marriage was the furthest thing from her mind, and that even if it wasn't, then she would be quite capable of choosing her own *mann*. She decided against it. What was the point? It would only make her *mudder* angry.

"Well, don't you think so?"

"*Jah, Mamm*. I mean, I guess so."

As Esther shelled the peas, she wondered why her *mudder* still held such a dislike for the Hostetler *familye*. Her *daed* had been able to forgive them, so why couldn't her *mudder*? Besides, the ministers always said that unforgiveness was a grave sin.

"*Mamm*, don't be angry with me, but I must say this."

Her *mudder* turned around with her nostrils flaring. "What is it?" she snapped.

"You know that I've gone on buggy rides with Jacob, don't you?"

Her *mudder* stood staring at her and said coldly, "What of it?"

"It's a little odd that you bring a boy to dinner when I'm going on buggy rides with another boy." Esther considered herself very brave by bringing the obvious to her *mudder*'s attention.

Her *mudder* didn't say a word, but turned back to stirring a pot on the stove. She stirred it a little too vigorously, causing the contents to spray out.

After Esther had helped her *mudder* in the kitchen

for a while, she heard the sound of a buggy. The buggy had to be Amos arriving for dinner. Esther had to admit she was a little pleased that he had arrived, not because she liked him, but because her *mudder* was giving her the silent treatment. The last half hour cooking in the kitchen with her *mudder* had been quite tense.

"I'll go let him in," Esther said to her *mudder*. Her *mudder* remained silent with the same fixed, stony expression on her face.

Esther hurried to the door, glad to have finally escaped her *mudder's* anger. "Come in, Amos."

"Nice to see you again, Esther."

Jah, 'Nice to see you again so very soon,' is what he should have said, Esther thought. *Amos has to think it odd that he's been asked for dinner again, and so soon.*

After Esther's *mudder* rang the dinner bell, everyone gathered around the table and took their seats. The dinner bell was an old, brass cow bell that Esther's *daed* had recently found in the fields and given to her *mudder*. The noise it made rather grated on Esther's nerves, but tonight was not the time to voice her views on the cow bell.

Esther wondered what on earth she could talk to Amos about, since she was sure she had exhausted everything that they could possibly talk about, the last time he was there for dinner. Thankfully, Amos and Martha seemed to be having a nice little chat amongst themselves.

Esther examined her *schweschder's* face as she

spoke to Amos. There was a definite sparkle in her eyes, and every now and then there was a little flutter of her eyelashes. It seemed to Esther that there was something happening between the two of them and she looked at her *mudder* to see if she had any inkling of what was happening.

As Esther caught her *mudder's* eye, her *mudder* interrupted Amos and Martha. "Amos, did I mention to you that Esther cooked the bean and beef casserole?"

A chill ran through Esther's body, and if she could have crawled under the table, she would have. It was an exact replica of the previous time that Amos had been invited to dinner, and no less embarrassing for the both of them.

"It's very *gut*, Esther," was Amos's polite reply, before he went back to speaking to Martha. "Can you cook well too, Martha?"

"I don't know how well I cook, but I'm going to have my own chocolate business."

Esther noticed her *mudder* moved uncomfortably in her seat. That was obviously not the response she was hoping for.

Esther was relieved when the time came for her to place the cheesecake and Shoo-fly pies on the table, as it signaled that dinner had nearly come to an end. She would not have too much longer to endure her *mudder's* enthusiastic matchmaking.

Later in the week, Esther was hanging out laundry. Black clouds were gathering in the sky, and Esther wanted the washing to dry before the storm hit.

Esther loved thunderstorms, the feeling of serenity in the air, the feeling of anticipation, and the change in the air's atmosphere.

Esther heard the sound of footsteps, and turned to see Jacob. Her heart always beat a little faster when Jacob was around.

"*Hullo*, Esther."

"*Hiya*, Jacob. You appeared out of nowhere. I didn't hear you drive up." She looked long and hard at Jacob. His usual smile was gone.

"I've been trying to get a break in work for a while to speak with you. I heard you had Amos over for dinner yet again."

Esther screwed up her nose. "*Jah*, my *mudder* invited him again."

Jacob looked down at his feet. "Doesn't she know about us? Haven't you told her?"

Esther stared into his face and saw that his usual crooked smile was replaced by a worried frown. "*Mamm* said he was here to visit his *schweschder*. Jacob, you look so worried. It's as if you think that we're dating for real." Esther laughed, and pinned a shirt on the line.

Jacob's head hung low.

"Jacob Hostetler, we are pretending to date and nothing more." *Surely he wasn't mistaken about our deal,* she thought. Nee, *of course he knew that we were pretending to date and nothing more.*

Jacob's chin came up. "*Jah*, of course I know that. I'm just thinking of you and making it real. If we were dating for real and your *mudder* kept trying to match you up with someone else, then I'd be upset, wouldn't I?"

Esther was ashamed of what she had just said to Jacob. He was trying to help her and she'd taken it the wrong way. "Forgive my harsh words, Jacob."

"No words that come from your mouth could ever be harsh, Esther."

Esther looked into his eyes as he spoke and she saw a gentleness that she had never seen in another person before. She considered that *Gott* had blessed her with a *gut* and kind friend.

Chapter Fourteen

Esther, her parents, her *schweschders,* Martha and Rebecca, and Mary arrived at the barn-raising at dawn, eager to help their neighbors, Albrecht and Lydia Glick, whose barn had been struck by lightning and had subsequently burned down.

Many buggies had already arrived and were parked along the side of the dirt road, their horses already unhitched and grazing in the field. The community's bench wagon was already there too, and men were unloading the tables and benches for the meals that would be served later in the day. Today the men would complete the whole timber frame structure of the new barn. The foundation had already been laid and the concrete had set.

The early morning mist eddied its way down the surrounding hills. Esther loved this time of morning. It always brought with it a promise of what the rest of the day could bring. She wondered what Jacob was doing, and then saw him. He was one of the *menner* already hammering away. A crane and operator had been hired, and Esther stared up at it for a few moments.

Esther and her *schweschders* helped their *mudder* unload the food they had brought with them: pans of roasting chicken, loaves of freshly baked bread, and countless pies. They carried all the containers of food into the Glicks' *haus*, where the women would spend the morning cooking.

It was quieter in the *haus*. The only sound outside was the noisy hammering. Rebecca set to work making ham and cheese sandwiches, while Martha and Mary helped other women peel potatoes for the mashed potatoes and potato salad to be served later. Esther got to work making pastry. She had to make a considerable amount of pastry, as many varieties of pies were planned: rhubarb pie, sour cherry pie, black walnut pie, sour cream raisin pie, lemon custard pie, and coconut custard pie.

Esther was busily rubbing the butter into the flour with her fingertips, when Jessie Yoder appeared at her shoulder, and looked at the large bowl. Esther was somewhat unnerved, but simply said, "*Hullo*, Jessie."

Jessie took the bowl from her. "You're doing that all wrong, Esther," she said. "You're taking too long. You'll make the dough hot, and you're squashing all the air out. It won't be light."

Esther knew she was doing it correctly. She had done it many times before and her pastry always turned out well. However, she did not want to argue with Jessie, so simply fetched another bowl, more flour and butter, and found a vacant spot on the other side of the kitchen. Soon Esther was kneading the pastry, but Jessie came over again. "Don't knead it so hard, Esther. You're overworking it. It's going to be tough."

Esther rolled her eyes. "Here, Jessie, how about you make the pastry, and I'll go and peel potatoes."

"Well, there's no need to be rude, Esther," Jessie said in a raised voice. "I was only trying to help." Jessie then strutted away.

All the ladies turned to look, and Beth Yoder, Jessie's mother, frowned at Esther disapprovingly. Esther wished she could sink through the floor—she was so embarrassed. She wished she could say, *It wasn't me! It was her*, but of course she couldn't.

Esther's morning did not improve. She was working near the hot oven, and the day was growing warmer. Jessie didn't speak to her again, but every time she glanced up, Jessie shot her an irritated look before looking away. Esther wished lunch would hurry, so she could go out into the fresh air to take food to the *menner*. Maybe she would have a chance to speak to Jacob. That would lift her spirits.

The morning passed quickly. With so much food to prepare, Esther barely had time to think. She helped the other ladies carry out vast amounts of food: roasted chickens, cold cuts, mashed potato, gravy, creamed celery, corn, applesauce, fruit salad, pickled relish, potato salad, coleslaw, tapioca pudding, and all manner of scrumptious pies and large tubs of ice cream and fruit salad.

Soon the munching sounds made by the *menner* were rivaled only by the munching sounds of the buggy horses in the field nearby.

Esther deposited platters of bread, butter, and jelly on the tables. She saw where Jacob was, and intended to go to his table next, but Jessie beat her to it. "Here you are, Jacob," she gushed, "I have a *schnitz und knepp* just for you. I know how much you like apples and dumplings. I made it just for you."

The *menner* at the table turned to look, and Albrecht Graber, who was sitting next to Jacob, gave Jacob a congratulatory pat on the back. Jacob hung his head and slid down on the bench a little. Esther stopped in her tracks. She had no wish to go over to Jacob now, not now that Jessie was there and making a scene. *How does she know what Jacob likes?* Esther thought, with a flash of irritation and perhaps a pinch of jealousy. *Well, I suppose Jessie's over at the Hostetlers'* haus *a lot. Besides, I full well know she didn't make that* schnitz und knepp *at all. It was one of the older ladies who made it.*

Jacob looked up and met her eye. His expression was pinched. Esther turned to another table, but too late realized that Amos was at that table.

"*Hiya*, Esther! *Wie gehts*?" His voice was loud and booming.

"*Hiya*, Amos. I'm *gut*, thank you. I have to go and get more bread." Esther scurried back to the *haus*, but not before she caught a glimpse of Jacob's troubled face.

When Esther arrived in the *haus*, the women were

grouped around Hannah. "I'm all right now," she protested. "It was just that the smell of the meat suddenly made me feel badly nauseous for some reason. I don't know why. Perhaps I'm coming down with the flu."

All the older women's hands flew to their mouths in unison. Mrs. Miller stepped forward, beaming widely. Esther couldn't remember the last time that she had seen her *mudder* look so pleased.

Esther and Hannah exchanged looks, and Hannah raised her eyebrows. "What's going on?"

"Silly child," her *mudder* scolded. "Maybe there's a *boppli* on the way, *jah*?"

Hannah sat down on the first available chair, a look of shock on her face. Mrs. Miller smiled over at Noah's mother, Katie Hostetler, who was also highly excited. *Perhaps this* boppli *will bring reconciliation between our* familyes, Esther thought, while still trying to take in the fact she might be an *aenti* one day soon.

Hannah held up a hand. "*Nee*, *nee*, it's too early to tell, really."

"Don't worry, we won't tell the *menner* yet," Mrs. Miller said. "Hannah, you should go home and rest."

"I'm not an invalid," Hannah protested, "and it's probably only the flu."

That brought muffled laughter from all the older women present.

Noah's *mudder*, Katie, stepped forward. "Your *mudder's* right, Hannah. Since the smell of the food is making you sick, you should go home and rest. I'll drive you."

Mrs. Miller nodded. "*Denki*."

Esther stared at her *mudder*. Had she actually thanked Mrs. Hostetler, and with genuine thanks too? Maybe *Gott* was already working through this *boppli*, although, as Esther reminded herself, no one was as yet certain that there was a *boppli* on the way.

With Hannah gone, Esther set herself to carrying out the pies that she had spent all morning making. She looked around but couldn't see Jessie, so headed straight for Jacob's table. Yet again, Jessie popped up as if from nowhere, and placed a pie directly in front of Jacob. "I know sour cherry pie is your favorite pie, Jacob, and I made it especially for you."

Esther felt as if she had a bad case of déjà vu, with Jessie's repeat performance. Jacob was slumping down in his seat, just like he did earlier.

"How was your *schnitz und knepp*, Jacob?" Jessie leaned right over Jacob.

"Go on," one of the men encouraged him, "tell her it was *appeditlich*." The *menner* all smiled. It was obvious to Esther than the *menner* at the table thought that Jacob and Jessie were courting, and this made her mad, so mad in fact, that she had to set her jaw and clench her teeth to stop saying anything. Esther would have liked to have said, *I made that sour cherry pie, not Jessie*, and, *He's mine! Stay away from him!*

It was only as she lay in bed that night, listening to the late rain beating rhythmically on the tin roof of the workshop, that she wondered why she was, in fact, so dreadfully upset about people thinking that Jessie and Jacob were courting.

Chapter Fifteen

Esther was sitting at the Hostetlers' kitchen table. For the first time since she had asked Jacob to fall in with her plan and pretend that they were dating, she felt bad. Throwing her own *mudder* off the track was one thing, but she had no wish to deceive the Hostetlers.

The Hostetlers appeared delighted that she was dating Jacob, a fact that made Esther feel even worse. Mrs. Hostetler had refused her offer of help with the dinner, so she sat talking to Mr. Hostetler, Jacob, and Jacob's two younger *bruders*, Moses and Elijah. They put her at her ease at once, and she enjoyed spending time with the happy *familye*.

Of course, it was easier as her sister, Hannah, was married to Noah, the oldest Hostetler boy, and Hannah worked part time for Mrs. Hostetler in her quilt store. After Mrs. Hostetler returned with beef soup with dumplings, she chatted for a while about Hannah and the quilt store, but the conversation was soon cut short by the clip-clop of hooves approaching the *haus*.

Mr. Hostetler turned to his wife, "Are you expecting anyone, Katie?"

"*Nee.*" Mrs. Hostetler shrugged.

Mr. Hostetler went outside, and soon returned with Jessie Yoder, who bounced into the room looking quite smug. "*Hullo*, Mrs. Hostetler. My *mudder* sent me over with this for you."

The whiff of cigarette smoke hung around Jessie, as did the fragrance of crushed peppermint leaves. Esther figured Jessie regularly covered the smell of cigarettes with peppermint, although it had not been so successful on this occasion.

"*Denki*, how kind of Beth." Mrs. Hostetler took the basket and looked inside. "Oh, lovely, walnut gingerbread. Please thank your *mudder* for me. Won't you have dinner with us?"

Esther's stomach churned. People visited each other at dinnertime without notice all the time, but this could not be a coincidence. Jessie Yoder had her sights firmly set on Jacob, and she was not going to make it easy for Esther. Esther suspected that Mrs. Hostetler was aware of Jessie's ploy, but it was the done thing in their community to invite people for dinner. Besides, she was sure she had noticed reluctance in Mrs. Hostetler's tone.

Jessie sat on the spare chair next to Jacob, opposite Esther. She sat a little too close to Jacob for Esther's liking, leaning in to him, and even Jacob gradually moved his chair a little further away from her.

Just look at her, Esther thought. *Could she be any more obvious? Doesn't she realize that Jacob likes me, not her?* Then Esther caught herself. *What am I thinking? I'm playing my part too well. I almost thought I was dating Jacob for real.* The thought that she was jealous for a moment unsettled her. *I do have an overactive imagination, like* Mamm *said,* she thought.

Jessie looked at Esther from under her eyelashes. "How is Amos?"

"Amos?" Esther wanted to snap, "How should I know?" but caught herself in time. Instead she said, "I don't know. I'm sure he's fine."

Jessie pulled a face. "Surely Amos can't be fine, because his house just burned down. How can anyone be fine just after their house burns down?"

Esther tried to think of something polite to say in response but was unable to do so.

"Lizzie visited my mother yesterday," Jessie continued. She glared at Esther.

"That's nice," Esther said, wondering what was coming next. Jessie looked like a cat about to pounce on a mouse. Esther's stomach muscles clenched involuntarily.

"Lizzie said Amos wants to marry you."

Esther saw Mr. and Mrs. Hostetler exchange glances. Jacob shifted uncomfortably in his seat.

Once more Esther was at a loss, but Jacob spoke up. "Surely Amos knows that Esther and I are courting."

Jessie shot him a look from under her lashes. "I

don't know what Amos thinks," she said evenly. "I only know what Lizzie told my *mudder*."

No one spoke. Esther continued to eat dumplings, hoping Jessie would stop talking. Unfortunately that was not the case.

"Lizzie thinks you secretly like Amos, but because your mother is pushing you into marriage with him, you are rebelling."

Esther went to make a hasty retort but caught herself just in time. "*Nee*, that's not true," she said. "I am not a rebellious person and I have no interest in Amos."

"Well, what else could you possibly say with Jacob here?" Jessie said snarkily.

"This talk is not appropriate," Mr. Hostetler said firmly, and Esther breathed a big sigh of relief. "Esther and Jacob are courting, so there will be no talk of other *menner*."

Jessie simply narrowed her eyes and continued to glare at Esther. The *familye* ate in silence, which Esther figured was due to Jessie's unsettling presence. It was well known throughout the community that Jessie had a crush on Jacob, and it looked as if she was going to put up a fight for him.

Jacob was not happy that Jessie Yoder had dropped in out of the blue. He didn't wish to be harsh with her, but he had never given her any hint that he returned her affections, yet she had been pursuing him for ages.

He also didn't appreciate the snide remarks she

frequently made about Esther. What's more, only the other day, Jessie had reported to him that Amos had been to the Millers again for dinner, and that Mrs. Miller had told her *gut* friend Beth, Jessie's mother, that Esther would marry Amos if she had anything to do with it.

Jacob felt his heart pinch when he thought about Esther marrying Amos. While he knew that Mrs. Miller could not force Esther to marry anyone, she could certainly apply plenty of pressure, and he had seen for himself just what a forceful person Mrs. Miller was.

He could see a future where he was married to Jessie, and Esther was married to Amos, and he didn't like that future one bit.

When the last piece of sour cherry pie had been polished off, Jessie stood up. "*Denki*, Mr. and Mrs. Hostetler. I'd better be going now, so I can help my *mudder*."

It was all Esther could do not to breathe a loud sigh of relief. She wouldn't have guessed that Jessie would leave the second that dinner was over. She had suspected Jessie would stay around for ages.

Esther's heart was steadying when seconds later, there was a loud yell. Everyone leaped to their feet and hurried outside. They found Jessie lying, crumpled, on the ground, at the bottom of the stairs.

Mr. Hostetler reached her first and helped her sit up. She clutched her ankle in a rather dramatic fashion, and then reached out her hands for Jacob. He looked around at everyone and then took a step closer to Jessie.

"I've broken my foot." Jessie made little crying sounds, but Esther couldn't see any actual tears. *I'm sure this is an all act to get Jacob's attention*, she thought, and then hoped she wasn't being unkind.

"Jacob, take me to the hospital."

Mrs. Hostetler came forward and spoke to her husband. "Take her into the *haus*, Reuben, and Moses, you can go fetch the *doktor*."

"*Nee*, *nee*, *nee*!" Jessie's screeches reached ear-splitting proportions. "*Nee*! It's broken, I tell you! Take me to the *doktor*!"

Mr. and Mrs. Hostetler exchanged glances. "All right then, I'll take you to the *doktor*," Mrs. Hostetler said.

"I'll go harness up Barney," Mr. Hostetler added, and hurried to the barn.

"*Nee*!" Jessie screeched again, reaching out her arms for Jacob. "I want Jacob to take me."

Jacob stood a step back and looked at Esther, his forehead furrowing into a deep frown.

"All right then. Jacob, take Jessie to the *doktor*." Mrs. Hostetler gave Jacob a sympathetic look as she said it. "Jessie, you had better not come around here again until your ankle is well and truly healed. I do not wish to be responsible for any more accidents."

Esther bit back a smile at Mrs. Hostetler's words. Her smile was short lived, however. As Mr. Hostetler brought the buggy up to where Jessie was sitting, Jessie flung her arms around Jacob's neck. He helped her stand up, but she collapsed back onto the ground. "It hurts! It hurts! You'll have to carry me, Jacob."

Jacob sighed out loud, and then bent down to pick up Jessie. He picked her up easily, and carried her the short distance to the buggy where he deposited her on the front seat. Esther would have admired his strength if it were not for the fact that she was distracted by her irritation with Jessie. She had been having a nice dinner with the Hostetler *familye*, and Jessie had ruined all that.

Before he drove off, Jacob called to Esther. "Sorry about this, Esther. I'll call on you tomorrow." With that, he clicked up Barney and they drove off in the direction of the *doktor's haus*.

Mrs. Hostetler put her arm around Esther's shoulders. "Come inside and wait for Jacob. I don't think it'll be long before he returns. I'm sure the *doktor* won't find much wrong with Jessie's ankle."

Esther nodded and allowed herself to be led back inside. She sat at the kitchen table while Mr. Hostetler, Moses, and Elijah went into the living room.

Esther sat wringing her hands while Mrs. Hostetler went to make some hot garden tea. *Surely Jacob isn't in love with Jessie?* she thought. *He didn't look too happy to have to take her to the* doktor's, *although it was obvious that she was faking that fall. What if Jacob and Jessie planned it all to have some time alone? What if Jacob is only helping me because he's a gut friend, and doesn't want to tell me that he's in love with Jessie? That would explain why Jessie is so angry with me*, she thought. A tight knot formed in the pit of her stomach.

Mrs. Hostetler placed a cup of steaming garden tea in front of Esther. "You're not worried, are you?"

Esther was puzzled. "About Jessie's ankle?"

Mrs. Hostetler smiled. "*Nee.* You're not worried about Jacob? He only has eyes for you, you know."

Esther felt a slow, hot flush travel up her cheeks. She sipped the tea to avoid having to look at Mrs. Hostetler, letting the mint refresh her.

"Now, don't you worry about Jessie," Mrs. Hostetler continued, apparently concerned about Esther's silence. "Jessie Yoder has been after my son for a long time now, but he's never given her any encouragement at all. He's always been in love with you."

Esther's hand flew to her mouth. *In love?* she thought. The room spun, and dizziness swept over her. Could it be true? And would Mrs. Hostetler really know what was going on in her son's mind? *If it is true*, she thought, *then I can't lead Jacob on. I'll have to stop pretending that I'm dating him.* At the same time, Esther could not deny that she was anxious about Jacob being away so long with Jessie. Could she, in fact, actually be jealous? And if she was jealous, did that mean that she was actually in love with Jacob after all?

Esther felt sick to the stomach. She fought the urge to run out the door to escape from her thoughts. *I will wait a little longer*, she thought. Two cups of garden tea later, and there was still no sign of Jacob. Esther's earlier thoughts of worrying that Jacob might be in love with her had well and truly gone, and had been replaced with more pressing feelings of anxiety. What if Jacob was in love with Jessie Yoder? *Oh please,* Gott, *help me to sort out my feelings for Jacob*, was her silent prayer, as she sat at the table, anxiously awaiting the sound of hoof beats.

When Jacob had not returned after some time, Esther said her goodbyes to the Hostetlers, with anxiety gnawing away in her stomach. She drove home under the light of the full moon, a beautiful, incandescent moon no longer obscured by clouds. Yet Esther was in no mood to appreciate the beauty of the night's moon. As she turned off onto a dirt road that had no streetlights, a rolling mist came in. The moonlight playing through the rising mist caused all sorts of shapes to form, some of which looked like goblins to Esther.

If only Jacob were here, she thought. *I always feel safe with Jacob.*

Yet would Jacob ever drive her anywhere again? Perhaps he was in love with Jessie Yoder. And if he hadn't been before, perhaps Jacob would realize his true feelings for Jessie now that she had been hurt. *She can't have been pretending to be hurt after all*, Esther thought, *given how long she was at the* doktor's. A thought occurred to her. *Of course, they weren't at the* doktor*'s at all. It was all a ruse to have time together.*

A tear trickled down Esther's cheek, and she clicked her horse on, encouraging him to trot faster, away from the phantoms of the mist and her own imaginings.

* * *

The *doktor* came out of his room and spoke to Jacob. "I can't find anything wrong with her ankle at all."

No surprise to me, Jacob thought. He stood up. "So, I'll drive her home now."

"*Nee*, Jacob," the *doktor* said. "Jessie insists that she's in terrible pain with the ankle. There's no swelling or any signs of injury in fact, but it would be remiss of me if I didn't send her on to the hospital to have it examined there. I'll call a taxi for you to take her."

Jacob sighed long and hard. It was bad enough that Jessie had ruined his dinner with Esther—and goodness knows what Esther was thinking—but now he had to go with Jessie to the hospital.

Once more, he was struck by the image of Esther married to Amos, and himself married to Jessie. He took a deep breath, and shook the image from his head. He wouldn't get ahead of himself. He'd simply wait for Jessie and push all thoughts of Amos from his mind.

Jacob sat in the hospital waiting room, looking at the bleak, pale green walls, and the tired nurses hurrying to and fro. Jacob had been waiting in the room for over two hours now. As Jessie's ankle wasn't swollen at all, and as the *doktor* hadn't found anything wrong with it, Jessie was at the bottom of a long list of patients in the emergency room.

Jacob wished he could go home and leave Jessie here, but her *familye* had not come to see how she was. *I bet her* mudder *is in on it too*, he thought bitterly. *And I will be lucky to get even an hour's sleep before I have to get up and start a hard day's work.*

Jacob was furious that Jessie had pretended to hurt her ankle, and he had absolutely no doubt that she had pretended. When would this ever end? The way she had clutched at him and insisted he drive her to the *doktor* just wasn't acceptable. He had been so looking forward to the dinner with Esther, and Jessie had ruined it, in more ways than one.

Chapter Sixteen

Esther woke up with a nasty, throbbing headache. She slipped groggily from bed and hurried down the stairs to make herself a mug of hot sage tea. Even the scent of the sage as she prepared the tea seemed to bring relief to the throbbing.

Her *mudder* was not around this morning as she was visiting Mrs. Troyer and helping with her chores for the day, so Esther was spared remarks and questions about her dinner at the Hostetlers' the night before.

With Martha and Rebecca busy doing the laundry, Esther set herself to baking. The headache had all but gone, and Esther had followed the sage tea with a mug of strong *kaffi*. She decided to make pumpkin pies as there were plenty of pumpkins. She didn't want to sew, as peering closely at the stitches could cause the headache to come back. The pile of mending would have to wait until later.

Esther was so busy cutting up pumpkins that she

didn't hear a buggy arrive, but she did hear a voice calling her from the front door. Esther hastily went to the door, the knife still in her hand.

Jacob poked his head around the door. "Can I come in?"

"Of course." Esther beckoned him in with the knife, her heart beating at a million miles an hour to see Jacob.

"Hey, steady on," Jacob said, with laughter in his voice. "It's not as if we're married already. No need to take a knife to me for driving another *maidel* to the *doktor's*."

Esther had to laugh, in spite of herself. "See that you never take another girl to the *doktor's* again, Jacob, or else." She laughed again. "Come on in, I'm making pumpkin pies."

Jacob rubbed his hands together.

"None ready for you, though. I'm still cutting up the pumpkins so the pies will be ages away. I'll make you some *kaffi*."

Esther poured coffee into two mugs, and sat down with Jacob at the kitchen table, after setting a plate of Shoo-fly pies between them. It was then she realized she hadn't asked after Jessie. Her overriding relief to see Jacob had driven all thoughts of good manners from her mind.

"So, how is Jessie's ankle?"

"Nothing wrong with it, as I suspected," Jacob said.

"You were a long while at the *doktor's* then, when there was nothing wrong with her ankle." Esther bit her lip. She hadn't meant the words to come out sounding like an accusation. Still, she had been up half the night worried that Jacob was in fact dating Jessie, and not wanting to tell her due to his desire to help save her from her *mudder's* matchmaking.

Jacob just looked at Esther strangely. He appeared to be choosing his words carefully, as he took a while before he spoke. "The *doktor* said that there was nothing wrong with her ankle, no swelling, no bruising, nothing at all, but Jessie kept clutching it, insisting that there was, so in the end the *doktor* said I should take her to the hospital to have it checked out. Anyway, long story short, a nurse assessed her and didn't think there was anything wrong either, so there was an awfully long wait before her ankle was X-rayed. I didn't get home until early this morning. Speaking of which, may I have another mug of *kaffi*?"

"Sure." As Esther poured him another mug of *kaffi*, she asked, "So the X-rays showed nothing was wrong?"

"*Jah*, nothing at all."

Esther nodded. "So Jessie was pretending to hurt her ankle so she could be alone with you." She said it as a statement, not a question. It was what she been convinced of all along.

Jacob fixed her with his crooked smile. "Well, I didn't want to say so myself, or you'd call me prideful again." He winked at her. "You'd better marry me soon with all those girls after me. That's the only sure way to keep them all at bay."

Esther forced a laugh. She didn't want Jacob to see what she really thought, and Jacob usually knew what she was thinking. Somewhere in the previous night, as she tossed and turned, she realized that she had fallen deeply in love with Jacob—or perhaps she had always loved him. One thing was certain, she could not bear the thought of Jacob being married to anyone else.

There was just one problem: Jacob only thought of her as a good friend.

"Anyway, why don't you come home with me for lunch?" Jacob continued. "My *mudder* put on some Dutch Cabbage Rolls before she went to the quilt store this morning. They'll be ready by the time we get home. I'll drive you and bring you back later."

Esther hesitated. It was so kind of Jacob to keep up appearances for her sake, but it was hard to be around him now that she knew her true feelings for him, given that he only thought of her as a friend. Still, she could not resist the opportunity to spend time with Jacob. "Sure," she said.

She looked up into Jacob's blue eyes and saw relief there. *Why would he be relieved that I'm coming to his* haus *for lunch?* she wondered.

Esther was quieter than usual on the buggy ride to the Hostetlers' farm. Jacob appeared to notice, as he kept looking her way.

When they arrived, Jacob drove straight to the barn and proceeded to unhitch his horse, Barney. Esther idly looked at the fresh-cut hay overflowing the storage mow. She loved the smell of hay, and even the pigeons that kept up their relentless cooing did not disturb her mood. She loved being so close to Jacob as he worked. A companionable silence settled between them.

"Jacob, *denki* so much for pretending that we're dating."

Jacob turned to her, a serious look on his face. "You're *wilkom*. I don't know if it's doing much good, though. Your *mudder* still seems to have her heart set on you dating Amos."

"*Ach*, she'll get over it sooner or later," Esther said, with more conviction than she felt.

Suddenly Jacob took Esther by the arm and led her out of the barn. "Come on, Esther. Let's have lunch."

As they walked out of the barn, Moses waved to them. "*Hiya*, Esther."

"*Hiya*, Moses."

Moses walked over. "Did you know that Jessie Yoder's here?" he asked.

"Do you know where she is?" Jacob looked over his shoulder.

"Somewhere around." Moses pointed to his left. "Her horse is tied up behind the barn. He's still hitched up. She said her *mudder* sent her with pies. I said I'd take them, but she said she'd wait for you and have lunch with you."

Jacob groaned. "More pies? Another meal? Did you tell her where I was?"

Moses nodded. "*Jah*, sorry, Jacob. I said you were bringing Esther back for lunch. I thought that would encourage her to leave, but it only made her want to stay. Anyway, I've got to run and help *daed*."

After Moses left, Jacob said, "I don't know what to do."

"Take me back home, please, Jacob." Esther didn't want to have another meal with Jacob with Jessie looking daggers at her.

"Are you sure?"

"*Jah*, it wouldn't be much fun."

Jacob stroked his chin. "I'll make it up to you, Esther."

Esther did not enjoy the ride back to her *haus* despite the fact she was alone with Jacob, and despite the fact that tingles ran through her at his close proximity. She was, in fact, plagued by too many questions. If Jacob had been really dating her, he wouldn't have driven her home, he would have firmly told Jessie that he was dating Esther and wanted to have lunch alone with her. The fact that they weren't *really* dating was irrelevant, as Jacob had been careful to keep up appearances previously. And what if Jacob was secretly seeing Jessie? That would explain Jessie's over-the-top behavior. Surely no girl would throw herself at a *mann* like that with absolutely no encouragement.

Jacob drove back from Esther's *haus*, upset that Jessie Yoder had ruined yet another time with Esther. *I'll have to put a stop to this somehow*, he thought. He also suspected he had seen Jessie in the barn, peering over the hay at him and Esther. He tried to remember what they'd been saying, as surely Jessie would have overheard.

When he got back to his *familye's* farm, he drove around to the back of the barn where Moses had said that Jessie's buggy was. It was nowhere to be seen. Jacob unhitched Barney, rubbed him down, and turned him out to graze, then went in search of Moses. He found him repairing a fence.

"Hey Moses, is Jessie still here?"

Moses stood up and shook his head. "*Nee*, she left right after you did."

Jacob shook his head in exasperation. "Well, why did she ruin my lunch with Esther?" He knew the answer, but was just speaking out of frustration.

Moses looked at Jacob for a minute before speaking. "This might sound unkind, but I think that Jessie will go to any lengths to keep you and Esther apart. She's a bit mean too—she was quite happy to tell me that Martha likes Amos Troyer."

Jacob was taken aback. "She did? Well, don't worry, Moses." He patted him on the shoulder. "I don't think Martha does, and besides, if her *mudder* thought she did, she wouldn't be trying to matchmake Amos with Esther, she'd be happy enough to matchmake him with Martha instead."

Moses looked downcast. "I hope you're right."

"Sure I am. Now I'll help you with this fence, and then I'll have to figure out what I'm going to say to Jessie Yoder. I need to have a talk with her."

Chapter Seventeen

Jacob stood in the store, looking at the vast array of clocks, wall clocks, table clocks, mantle clocks, and grandfather clocks. They all looked manly, though, and he was sure there was not one in sight that Esther would like. He had decided to buy an engagement gift for Esther, and typically engagement gifts were either clocks or china. The fact that Esther had not yet shown any interest in him as a *mann*, of course concerned him, but he had loved Esther all his life, and was determined to move forward until Esther was his *fraa*.

One little clock caught Jacob's eye. He knew how much Esther loved wood, and this was a pretty mahogany. The store owner hurried over to point out the clock's attributes, which Jacob soon heard featured *movingue* overlays and rare mahogany coupled with bronze feet. What's more, he was told, it had triple chime action.

Jacob rubbed his chin. "It's a gift, and she doesn't like noisy bells, so I doubt she'd like a chiming clock."

The store owner was unperturbed. "It's perfect then, as it has a chime silence option."

Jacob tuned out as the store owner went on at some length about the attributes of the various clocks. Jacob did not find clocks at all interesting, but he did think Esther would like that one clock. Still, he should go and look at china. Jacob was undecided, but then he thought he should buy Esther the little clock and perhaps china as well, if he could find a piece that she'd like.

He was leaving the store when he happened across Albrecht Graber, one of the *menner* who had been sitting with him for lunch at the barn-raising.

"*Hullo*, Jacob." Albrecht winked at him. "In the market for a clock?"

Jacob laughed, although he was a little uneasy that he had been seen looking at clocks, and by Albrecht Graber of all people. Albrecht could talk the leg off an iron pot, and wasn't known for his discretion. At any rate, being seen looking at clocks was the same as an *Englisch* man being seen looking at engagement rings. Jacob edged the box with the clock under his coat, although he was sure that Albrecht had already seen it, and that could mean it would soon be all over town. "And you?"

"Could be." Albrecht, a pleasant young *mann*, turned bright red and couldn't look Jacob in the eye.

Jacob wondered who the object of Albrecht's affections could be, and remembered that he had seen

Albrecht driving Sarah Hilty home after the most recent Singing. Jacob smiled. Albrecht and Sarah would make a lovely couple. The two said their goodbyes, and Albrecht went into the store while Jacob walked down the street to an antique store.

The china gift was supposed to be practical, and Jacob could not see any practical china in the antique store. He saw delicate teapots as well as cup and saucer sets in fine china, all of which looked as if they would break at the very first opportunity. Jacob wondered, if they truly were antiques, how they had survived so long. Jacob spent longer than he thought in the musty antique store, for he was distracted by a variety of fascinating antique tools.

Jacob gave up and decided to return home, but as he was on his way back, he passed a little specialty coffee store which featured exotic teas and coffees in the window. But what caught his eye was a teapot adorned by cats. Esther had always wanted a kitten, and she loved her meadow tea. This gift would be ideal for her.

Jacob stood and looked. The teapot was sturdy enough. Some in the community would consider it too ornamental, but Esther would love it. Besides, Esther's *daed's familye*, like his own *familye*, was not as strict as most of the other *familyes* in the community. Esther's *mudder's familye*, however, was from one of the strictest, and he figured she would not approve. Yet what mattered most to him was that Esther herself would love the little teapot.

Who am I fooling anyway? Jacob asked himself.

I'm ab im kopp, *crazy. Esther's never going to marry me. She's going to marry Amos.* And so, struck with indecision, Jacob stood, looking in the window at the little teapot, with the clock under his arm. *I expect I'll get married one day,* he thought sadly, *and whoever she is, I'll give her this clock, so it won't be wasted.*

Then his mind changed again. He remembered his *daed's* favorite saying, *"Guut gewetzt iss halwer gemaeht." Well begun is half done.*

I'll buy the teapot, he thought. *What can it hurt? I won't give up Esther without a good fight.*

Jacob went into the store and asked to see the cat teapot. The label said that it held four cups of tea. That meant one for him, one for Esther, and one each for two of their *kinner* when they were old enough to drink tea. Jacob blushed furiously at the thought. *I'm getting way ahead of myself here*, he silently scolded himself.

He paid for his purchase, and the elderly man behind the counter went to look for paper to wrap it up. He had just started to wrap it when Albrecht Graber walked through the door. Jacob wished the elderly man would wrap faster, before Albrecht saw it, but that was not to be.

"A teapot, Jacob?" he asked.

Jacob saw no way to deny it, so simply nodded.

"And you bought a clock as well, didn't you? I feel bad, as I didn't know whether to buy a clock or not, but I couldn't decide, so now I've come here looking for china for Sarah." Albrecht immediately looked horrified and put his hand over his mouth. "Oh no, me and my big mouth! You won't tell anyone, will you? My *mudder* always says I should think before I speak. Oh dear."

Jacob hastily assured the kindly Albrecht that he wouldn't tell a soul. Although at the same time, he was just as certain that Albrecht would probably let slip that he had seen Jacob buying a clock and china.

Chapter Eighteen

Esther hadn't seen Jacob for a whole week. This was not unusual for a dating couple in her community, and she was sure that he was kept busy on the farm. Nevertheless, she could not help but worry. After all, it was hard not to feel scared when Jessie was after Jacob.

One sunny morning, Esther was in the vegetable garden picking some sage for the stuffed acorn squash she was about to make, when she heard the clip-clop of hooves. She looked up in delight, hoping to see Jacob's buggy, but instead, Jessie Yoder's buggy drove into view.

Whatever is she doing here? Esther thought, and anxiety gnawed away at her stomach.

Jessie pulled her horse up. "*Hiya* Esther, can I speak with you?"

"Sure," Esther said with a strong feeling of dread. "Tie up your horse and we'll go into the *haus*."

"*Nee*, please stay here. I want to speak with you

in private." Esther nodded, and Jessie got out of her buggy.

This can't be good, Esther thought, with growing apprehension.

Jessie narrowed her eyes at Esther. "Esther, I wanted to apologize to you. I've been acting funny around you, and I wanted to tell you why, although I'll be in trouble for doing so."

"I don't understand," Esther said, trying to calm her anxiety.

"It's not easy to tell you." Jessie smiled, but Esther thought that the smile did not reach her eyes.

After Jessie hesitated somewhat, Esther asked, "What is it?"

A calculating look passed over Jessie's face. "It's about you and Jacob pretending to be a dating couple."

Esther's hand flew to her mouth. "But, but," she stammered, "how did you know?"

Jessie looked at Esther as if she were a complete idiot. "Well, Jacob told me, of course."

Esther looked at Jessie in utter shock.

"And I need your help."

"My help?" This was all too much for Esther. She sat down in the rich earth between the neat rows of vegetables and put her head in her hands. Esther was heartbroken. *It must be true*, she thought. The only other person in the world who knew about the secret was Jacob, so he must have told Jessie. But why? Why would he betray her trust?

Jessie stood over Esther, looking down at her.

"I know you and Jacob are pretending to be dating so your *mudder* won't pressure you to date Amos Troyer," she continued, her eyes narrowed.

Esther stood up, and leaned against the little white picket fence that protected the vegetables from the chickens. Her head was spinning—her whole world was spinning.

"The thing is, Esther," Jessie said, shooting Esther a calculating look, "that Jacob is secretly dating me."

Esther gasped at that piece of news and clutched at the fence with both hands. *It can't be true*, she thought.

"It's a secret as we don't want my *mudder* to find out. You know what *Mamm's* like! She doesn't like the Hostetler *familye* any more than your *Mamm* does. Jacob was about to tell you that we were dating the very day when you asked him to pretend to be dating you."

A wave of nausea swept over Esther. Her worst fears were being realized. This was exactly what she had been afraid of. She thought of Job's words from the Old Testament, "For the thing which I greatly feared is come upon me, and that which I was afraid of is come unto me." *Why are You testing me like this,* Gott*?* Esther caught her breath, doing her very best not to cry.

Jessie was still talking. "Jacob didn't want to hurt your feelings by telling you that he couldn't help you, as he wants to support you against being paired off with Amos. You *are* his good friend after all. The only problem is, that it hurts my feelings that Jacob is pretending to date you. You can understand that, can't you?"

Esther did her best to nod. She avoided Jessie's eyes.

Jessie leaned into her. "Esther, Jacob can't know that we've had this conversation. He didn't want to tell you, obviously. He really wants to help you."

Esther cleared her throat. "What do you want me to do?"

Jessie looked at her from below her narrowed lids. "Tell Jacob there's no need to pretend to be dating any longer. Tell him you like Amos after all—tell him anything you like, but he'll feel bad and he'll argue with you, so you'll have to make it convincing."

Esther stood there, dumbstruck, but Jessie pressed on. "You can't let him know I've told you," she said again, "because he'll be angry with me. This is our secret. I know this puts you in a difficult position, but your *mudder* can't *force* you to date Amos, so it's not all that bad, is it?"

Esther finally found her voice. "I suppose not," she croaked. Her mouth had suddenly gone dry.

"*Gut*!" Jessie exclaimed. "Then Jacob and I can keep dating in secret. Esther, you can't let on that you know about us dating, either. I know we haven't been friends in the past, but it's good of you to help me out like this. You will help me out, won't you? You will tell Jacob to stop pretending that he's dating you, won't you?"

"*Jah*." Tears pricked at Esther's eyes.

Jessie climbed back in her buggy and drove off,

leaving Esther standing there. Esther sank to the ground amidst the cucumbers and cried heartily, not caring one bit that she was sitting in the dirt and that her dress was newly washed. Laundry was the furthest thing from her mind. *It must be true*, she thought, *or how else would Jessie know? It must be true! Jacob and Jessie must be dating after all.* Her whole body was racked with sobs.

Esther hurried back into the *haus* to wash her face before her *schweschders* Martha and Rebecca saw her. Her face felt puffy, and her eyes were sore and irritated. For once, Esther wished she had a mirror so she could see just how bad she looked. It would be good to have some forewarning before she faced the inevitable barrage of questions from her *schweschders*. At least her *mudder* wasn't there, at any rate—she was in the basement doing the laundry.

As Esther emerged from the bathroom, Rebecca called from the kitchen. "Did you get the sage? You were ages."

Esther walked into the kitchen, taking deep, slow breaths. "Oh, I forgot it. I don't feel much like making the stuffed acorn squash now, anyway. I'll make it later."

"*Gut*, Martha and I are going to make apple pies. Can you do the pastry? You're much better at it than we are." Rebecca had her head down, peeling apples.

Just then Martha burst into the *haus* and hurried into the kitchen. "Was that Jessie Yoder?" she called out. Martha gasped when she saw Esther's face. "Esther, you've been crying," she exclaimed.

Rebecca turned to Esther. "What happened? Did Jessie Yoder make you cry? Oh goodness, and your dress is all dirty!"

They both put their arms around Esther's shoulders. The display of sympathy made Esther want to sob all over again, but she bit her lip and did her best not to cry. "I'm okay, really. Now are we making pastry?"

Martha peered into Esther's face. "Esther, you can tell us, really. Whatever happened? What did Jessie say? Did someone die?"

"*Nee*, no one died." As much as Esther wanted to share the burden with her younger *schweschders*, she could not. She hadn't told them in the first place that Jacob was pretending to date her, and then, being unsure of her feelings at the time, she had denied that she was in love with Jacob. It was all too complicated, and she wasn't up to explaining anything in depth.

"What happened, then?" Rebecca insisted.

Esther sighed deeply. "All I can tell you is that Jessie told me something that made me cry. It's her secret, though, so I'm not allowed to tell anyone."

Martha and Rebecca groaned in unison. "Why not?" they both said.

"It wouldn't be right. Now, Martha, take these sugar cookies out to *Datt* and Noah." She handed Martha a plate of soft, lightly browned cookies.

Martha leaned close to Rebecca. "Best not ask her any questions while I'm over at the workshop. She seems too upset," she whispered.

"I can hear you, Martha; I'm standing right here." Esther was amused, despite her broken heart.

Martha just smiled, and left with the cookies. "I bet she eats some cookies on the way over there," Rebecca muttered to herself. "Esther, do you want to sit down? I'll make you a nice cup of meadow tea."

"*Nee*, *denki*, it's best I keep busy." Esther poured some flour into a bowl.

"You'd better change your dress before *Mamm* sees it. She'll want to know why it's all dirty," Rebecca said.

"*Gut* idea." Esther looked down at the dress that had dirt all over the sides and back. "I'll go back for the sage first, and then I'll change."

Esther wiped the flour off her hands onto her apron, and hurried back to the vegetable garden.

The vegetable garden was neat and ordered. *I wish my life was so neat and ordered*, Esther thought sadly, looking at the well-organized rows of vegetables. Esther looked up at the beautiful, purple-feathered martins sitting on their martin houses. She remembered the Bible passage, *Are not two sparrows sold for a farthing? and one of them shall not fall on the ground without your Father. But the very hairs of your head are all numbered. Fear ye not therefore, ye are of more value than many sparrows.*

The words comforted Esther, and she sent up a silent prayer. "Please *Gott*, help me. No one can but You." It wasn't a long prayer, but it was a heartfelt one.

No sooner had she said the words than she saw a

buggy approaching from the distance. *I hope Jessie hasn't come back*, she thought, with a sick feeling in the pit of her stomach. As the buggy grew closer, Esther recognized it as Jacob's buggy—Jacob, the last person on earth she wanted to see. *Why,* Gott, *why?* she lamented. *The ministers said You wouldn't test us more than we can bear.*

Esther walked out of the vegetable garden and shut the gate behind her. Jacob climbed down from the buggy and tied his horse to the hitching ring.

"*Hiya*, Esther." Jacob's wide smile soon turned to a frown. "Esther, what's wrong?"

"Nothing." Esther could barely speak. Jacob was wearing his simple work clothes and had his usual crooked grin on his face. Esther's heart leaped.

Jacob stepped toward her. "Esther, it looks like you've been crying."

Esther shook her head. "*Nee*, it's just a cold."

Jacob's face was full of concern. "Are you okay?"

Esther nodded.

"Well, since our dinner was ruined last week," he continued, "I came to see if you'd like to come on another buggy ride with me."

Esther felt cold all over. Her limbs suddenly grew heavy. "It's okay, Jacob. You don't have to pretend anymore."

Jacob looked stunned. "What do mean?" He tilted his head to one side.

Esther drew a deep breath. "I'm very grateful to you, Jacob, for trying to help me by pretending we were dating, but there's no need to anymore."

Jacob's brow creased in a frown. "What's happened?" When Esther didn't answer, he continued, "Has your *mudder* stopped trying to matchmake you with Amos?"

Esther bit her lip.

"You're not interested in Amos now, are you?"

Esther suspected that she detected a hint of jealousy in Jacob's tone. *He's dating Jessie Yoder, so how can he be jealous of Amos?* she thought, frowning and crossing her arms.

"We just don't need to pretend anymore, Jacob. Can't you leave it at that?" Esther realized that she was sounding a little hysterical, but she didn't care too much just how high-pitched her voice came out.

"Esther, if you were seeing someone else, you'd tell me, wouldn't you?"

Jacob looked so upset, but Esther couldn't figure why. His question made things difficult for her. She felt she couldn't break Jessie's confidence, but Jacob was a dear friend and she didn't want to lie to him. After all, it was with him, not Jessie, that her loyalties lay.

"*Nee*, I'm not seeing anyone, Jacob," Esther said in a small, flat voice.

"But why then? I thought we, we…" Jacob's voice broke off. He looked at the ground for a moment.

"I have to go." Esther ran into the *haus*, leaving a stunned Jacob standing there.

Chapter Nineteen

Jacob was distraught. Esther was acting weirdly, and he didn't know what to make of it. She said she wasn't interested in any other *mann*, and he knew that Esther wouldn't lie to him, but something was badly wrong. For a moment he wondered if it was something to do with Amos, but that was nonsense. She would have said. Yet Esther had also been crying. Jacob felt helpless. He had no idea what he could do.

Jacob walked over to the workshop, and was greeted by the kindly Mr. Miller.

"*Hullo*, Jacob, you're looking for Noah?"

"*Jah*, I need his wisdom."

Mr. Miller waved a marking gauge in the direction of the door. "He finished up early today. You've just missed him. He'd be at his *haus* by now, working on a piece for me in his little workshop."

"*Denki*, Mr. Hostetler."

Jacob went to leave, but Mr. Miller called him

back. "Jacob, Martha brought us some cookies over before, and told us that Esther had been crying."

"Do you know why?"

Mr. Miller put the marking gauge down and took a step closer to him. "*Jah*. Well, not the precise reason, but Martha told us that Jessie Yoder had said something that made Esther cry," he said in lowered tones, although there was no one around to hear.

Jacob frowned.

"I saw Jessie Yoder over here earlier," Mr. Miller added, "talking to Esther when she was in the garden."

Jacob's chin was set hard. "Did she now! *Denki*, Mr. Miller, *denki* so much."

Jacob walked back outside. He debated whether to go to Esther now and tell her that he knew Jessie had said something to upset her, but Esther might not want to talk about it. As much as he wanted to pull Esther into his arms and soothe away whatever had upset her, he had better not act rashly. Noah would know what to do. Noah always knew what to do.

It was only a short drive to Noah and Hannah's *haus*, but it seemed to take forever. Jacob had to resist the urge to push his horse faster. When he arrived, he threw the reins over the tie rail and hurried through the open door into the garage that Noah had converted into a little workshop. Noah's horse neighed to Jacob's horse in greeting.

Noah looked up. "*Hiya*, Jacob. Is something wrong?" he added, taking in Jacob's appearance.

"*Jah*, a lot's wrong."

Noah looked Jacob up and down. "I can see that! You've gone as white as a ghost. Why don't you tell me about it?"

Jacob sat on the edge of the workbench and poured out the whole story, from Esther suggesting that they pretend to be dating, right up to the day's events, including the fact that Esther was crying after a visit from Jessie Yoder, while Noah listened patiently.

"So, what do you make of all that?" he asked Noah urgently when he finished.

Noah rubbed his newly growing beard. "Well, there's only one logical explanation," he said slowly.

Jacob held his breath, anxiously waiting to hear Noah's words. Right then Hannah's tan and white beagle puppy, Annie, bounced up and seized him by the trouser leg. "Ouch," he yelled. "She bit me."

Noah did his best not to laugh. "She's just being a puppy."

"*Jah*, but it hurts just the same." Jacob removed his trousers from the razor sharp teeth of the enthusiastic puppy. "So, what were you going to say?" Jacob looked around for something to put in the puppy's mouth. He found a pink, plush elephant and stuck it in Annie's mouth. That did the trick, as Annie happily sat down and crunched on the toy.

Squeak, squeak, squeak. Jacob had no idea that the pink elephant was a squeak toy. He shook his head. This just wasn't his day.

"Jessie's doing her best to break up you and Esther, right?" Noah said the words loudly to be heard over the squeaks, which were coming one on top of the other.

Jacob nodded furiously. "*Jah*, but we're only pretending that we're dating."

"That doesn't matter. Jessie knows how you feel about Esther. Esther is in love with you, and…"

Jacob interrupted him. "I wish that were the case, Noah, but she isn't."

Noah wagged his finger at him. "I think you'll find, little *bruder*, that she is. Why else would she be so upset? What do you think Jessie said to her that upset her so much? And more of a clue, what did Jessie say to her that made Esther tell you, right after that, that you didn't have to pretend to date her anymore? It's obvious. Esther's in love with you."

Jacob put his hand to his mouth. "Do you really think so? I mean, I hope so, but I don't think she was before."

Noah chuckled. "I think she always was, Jacob, but perhaps she's just now realized it."

Jacob ran his hands through his hair. "What do you think Jessie said to her?"

"She likely said that she was dating you, or that you were interested in some other girl, but knowing Jessie, she probably said that you and she were dating."

Jacob tried to take it all in. It had been such an eventful day, and his head was reeling from the events. "What should I do now, Noah?"

"You need to go to Esther and tell her that you're not dating Jessie, and ask Esther to marry you."

Jacob sucked in a deep breath. "But that will be embarrassing if she doesn't want me after all."

Noah laughed. "I think you're on safe ground, Jacob. Trust me." When Jacob didn't look convinced, he added, "What's the alternative? You really don't have a choice."

Jacob shrugged his shoulders. "You're right. I really do need to have a talk with Jessie Yoder, though. I need to tell her that I'm in love with Esther and that I won't tolerate any more of her troublemaking."

"Tell her you'll go to the bishop if she causes any more trouble."

Jacob nodded. "*Gut* idea. That's likely the only thing that'll stop her."

Jacob drove to the Yoders' *haus*, nervous about speaking to Jessie Yoder, but happy that he at least had a plan. He hoped he would be able to speak to Jessie alone, and that her *mudder* would not be nearby.

Jessie must have seen him coming, as she was waiting for him on the road outside her *haus*. Jacob hopped out of the buggy and tied his horse. His first thought was that Jessie looked worried.

"She's told you, hasn't she?" she snapped.

"Esther?"

"*Jah*, of course. She told you what I said to her." Jessie's fists were clenched and she looked furious.

I'll play along with her, Jacob thought. *I might get more out of her that way, if she thinks I already know.* "*Jah*, she did, and I'm not happy about it," he said.

Jessie's face formed into a pout. "She said she wouldn't tell you."

"Why did you say it, Jessie?" Jacob hoped he was asking the right questions to get Jessie to reveal what she'd said to Esther.

Jessie looked at Jacob through narrowed eyes. "Well, I overheard what the two of you said in the barn."

Aha, so she was there after all, Jacob thought. "What did we say?"

Jessie jutted out her chin. "You said you were pretending to be dating, so if you were only *pretending* that you were dating, I thought it wouldn't do any harm."

"What wouldn't do any harm, Jessie?" Jacob's patience was running out.

"I told Esther that you told me that you two were pretending to be dating."

"And that's not all, is it, Jessie?" Jacob wasn't sure, but he wanted to know if there was more.

Jessie couldn't meet his eyes. "Well, I might have told Esther that you and I were secretly dating."

Jacob couldn't believe it. He was annoyed at Jessie, and sad that she had upset Esther, yet it was clear to him now that Esther must have feelings for him. Why else would she have cried after being told that he was dating Jessie?

"She promised she wouldn't tell," Jessie snapped. "She's a liar."

"You will *not* speak about Esther that way, Jessie Yoder," Jacob said firmly. "And Esther didn't tell me. I'd heard she was upset and so I came here to find out."

"Oh but you said..." Jessie broke off, and then continued. "Oh, you tricked me." Her tone was resigned.

"*Jah*."

"And you didn't speak to Esther?"

"*Nee*. Now Jessie, there will be no more trouble-making, do you understand?"

Jessie pulled a sulky face.

"Jessie, if you do one more thing to cause trouble between me and Esther, if you turn up uninvited at my *haus* one more time, or if you speak to Esther, I'll go to the bishop."

Jessie gasped. "You wouldn't."

"*Jah*, I would."

Jacob saw a calculating look pass across Jessie's face. "I mean it, Jessie." Jacob made his voice as stern as he could. "I mean it. Even if you break your leg, I will not be the one to drive you to the *doktor*. Do you understand?"

"Sure," Jessie said with a smirk.

Chapter Twenty

Esther was not looking forward to going to Jessie Yoder's birthday party. She had completely forgotten about it, given all the excitement over the Troyers' house fire and Lizzie staying with them. Mrs. Miller had already selected a gift from the entire family.

Esther knew she would have to go and pretend everything was fine, but she did not want to see Jacob and Jessie together.

Mrs. Miller called out to the girls. "Hurry, all of you. Beth will be upset if we're late. She is not partial to tardiness."

Esther, Martha, and Rebecca came down the stairs. "We're ready, *Mamm*," Martha said.

"Good. Now to collect Lizzie and Mary."

As the women walked down the steps of the Millers' house, Lizzie and Mary came around the corner. Mary looked downhearted, and Esther hoped Lizzie had not said something to upset her again.

"You'll see Pirate again soon," she said to Mary to cheer her up.

Her words had the desired effect. Mary beamed from ear to ear. "I can't wait to see him."

The women piled into the buggy and Mrs. Miller took the reins. "I don't know why you took so long, girls," she complained. "The poor horse has been standing in the sun for a full five minutes since I harnessed him up."

Esther knew her mother was exaggerating, but it certainly wouldn't do to point that out.

The buggy set off at a good pace toward the Yoders' farm. A dark cloud had descended over Esther. She would have to get used to seeing Jessie and Jacob together, but that didn't mean she would like it. Her heart was broken.

Mary chatted all the way to the Yoders' house, which seemed to annoy Lizzie, whereas Mrs. Miller didn't seem to mind at all.

"How exciting, a birthday party for Jessie," Mary said. "I don't think she likes me though. I think she thinks I talk too much."

"I can't imagine why," Lizzie said snarkily.

"Of course you don't talk too much, Mary," Mrs. Miller snapped.

Esther wondered if her mother's words were meant to serve as a deliberate rebuke to Lizzie, and even wondered if Lizzie was beginning to get on her mother's nerves. Certainly, her mother was fond of Mary.

Mary smiled and nodded and continued to talk. "I

like birthday parties, all the gifts and cards and the good food. I wonder what we'll have to eat?"

Lizzie opened her mouth and then abruptly shut it. Esther wondered if Lizzie was going to say something about the amount of food Mary ate but then thought better of it after what Mrs. Miller had just said.

"And I can't wait to see Pirate too," Mary gushed. "David is doing an awfully good job with him. You wouldn't think he was the same dog we found. I'm so pleased his owners never came to collect him."

"I suspect his owners were not looking for him," Mrs. Miller said. "I suspect they didn't want the dog and that's why he was wandering around."

"How could people do that?" Mary said. "Besides, he's a lovely dog. Sure, he mightn't be the best looking dog in the world, but it is what is inside that counts, isn't it?"

"It sure is," Esther said lazily, wishing she could enjoy the breeze and the scenery as she once did before she found out about Jacob and Jessie. It was as if her heart had turned into a large lump of coal. Would she ever love another man? Would she end up alone, without *kinner*, and bitter like Lizzie? Esther sure hoped not, but that was certainly the way it was looking.

"Esther!" Mrs. Miller snapped.

Esther gave a little start. "Sorry, *Mamm*. Did you say something?"

"Yes, I asked you again and again if you remembered to bring the pumpkin pie for Beth?"

"Yes I did," Esther said.

"*Gut.*"

"I wonder if Jessie will like our gift?" Mary said. "Oh, please forgive me, Mrs. Miller. I meant no offense. Of course she will like the gift because you chose it, after all. It's such a lovely gift and so thoughtful too."

"It's always the thought that counts with gifts," Lizzie said in a stern tone.

"Yes, it's the thought that counts, but it's also nice if you get a gift that you actually like, isn't it?" Mary said.

Lizzie simply glared at her.

Esther poked one finger under her prayer *kapp* and scratched her head. She certainly hoped the conversation on the way home would be less tense, but she imagined it would be even worse after she had seen Jacob and Jessie together. It was too much for her to bear. If only she could have pretended to be sick and stayed home.

When they finally reached the Yoders' house, several buggies were already there. "I know we're late," Mrs. Miller said. "Next time we're going somewhere you girls will have to be ready. I don't know what takes you so long when all you have to do is change your dresses and wash."

Rebecca and Martha exchanged glances while Esther rubbed her temples. A throbbing headache was coming on. She would have to ask Beth Yoder for some peppermint to rub on her temples.

When the women got down from the buggy, Mary

was visibly upset. "Where is Pirate?" she said. "I hope nothing's happened to him. I can't see him."

David walked around the side of the barn. "Where's Pirate?" Mary called to him.

"He's fine," David said. "*Mamm* told me to tie him in the barn because he's not used to so many people. There hasn't been a meeting here since we got Pirate so he probably isn't used to crowds."

Mary's shoulders relaxed. "*Jah*, that's a good idea. Good thinking of your mother's." She let out a long slow sigh of relief.

"Do you want to come and see him?" David asked her, but before she could answer, he added, "We can't throw sticks to him because he has to say tied up until everyone leaves."

Mary nodded and hurried over to David. The two of them disappeared inside the barn.

Esther looked around. It did seem as though they were the last to arrive. Esther gasped when she recognized Mrs. Hostetler's buggy. She had thought Mrs. Hostetler would be at work and now she was worried about how her mother would react. However, her mother had been much nicer to Mrs. Hostetler since the news that Hannah was having a *boppli*.

Beth Yoder greeted them warmly, holding open the door for everyone to enter. Jessie was sitting on a couch looking like the cat that got the cream. *Don't be so mean*, Esther silently scolded herself. *It's her birthday. I have to be nice to her. Besides, she can't help it that I'm jealous of her relationship with Jacob.*

And where was Jacob? Esther looked around, but

could not see him. Mrs. Hostetler walked over to her. "I had to come as my sons weren't able to come today," she said. "They all had to work and weren't able to get away."

Esther nodded slowly.

"Jacob says to say *hullo*."

"Please tell him I said *hullo* too," Esther said, rather puzzled. Didn't Mrs. Hostetler know about Jacob and Jessie? Then again, Jessie had said it was a secret, so maybe it was a secret even from Jacob's mother.

Esther didn't know how she felt about Jacob's absence. On the one hand, it was good she wouldn't be pained seeing Jessie and Jacob together, but on the other hand, a small part of her wanted to see if it really was true. Part of her couldn't quite believe that Jacob, *her* Jacob, and Jessie were really dating.

Jessie was already opening a gift, so Esther figured people would give her their gifts and then everyone would eat. She hoped Jessie wouldn't gloat about dating Jacob, but since it was clearly a secret relationship, she figured Jessie wouldn't. That afforded Esther a small measure of relief.

Mrs. Hostetler's gift was next. She handed it to Jessie. "How lovely, a quillow," Jessie said. "*Denki*, Mrs. Hostetler. It is beautiful and will be lovely for when I'm married."

She looked directly at Esther when she said it. Esther knew those words were not said at random—they were words meant directly for her. It seemed

Jessie wasn't about to play nice and spare her feelings after all.

Jessie looked at the card and then put a hand over her heart. "What beautiful thoughts. Please thank Jacob for me." She plastered what Esther thought was meant to be a sweet expression on her face.

Katie Hostetler was clearly puzzled. "Why, the card is from the whole Hostetler *familye.*"

Jessie nodded slowly. "Sure," she said, and then winked at Esther.

Esther wanted to get away as far from Jessie as possible, but she was stuck in the Yoders' house with her and there was nothing she could do about the situation.

David and Mary hurried through the door. "Not late, am I?" Mary said breathlessly. "I'm sorry I took so long patting Pirate. He doesn't seem to mind being tied up, although he'd rather chase sticks, of course. Well, he is a dog, after all. I'm not complaining about him being tied up, you realize, Mrs. Yoder. Mrs. Miller, you haven't given Jessie our gift yet, have you?"

Mrs. Miller shook her head. "Of course not. I was waiting for you."

"*Denki.*" Mary sat on a spare chair and folded her arms in her lap.

"Here is our gift," Mrs. Miller said, handing Jessie a large box.

Jessie opened it and exclaimed in delight. "A seven piece glass and pitcher set! *Denki*, Mrs. Miller and all of you. You too, Mary. This will be ideal for when I'm married." She shot Esther a sideways look.

Lizzie walked over and handed her a box of coconut macaroons. "I made these for you. I wasn't able to get you anything else, with, well you know, not after the fire."

Jessie accepted the coconut macaroons with what seemed to Esther to be genuine delight. "Lizzie, you shouldn't have got me anything at all, not after your fire. It is so good for you to do this for me. I'm grateful. *Denki*."

Esther realized Jessie's words were genuine. *She must have some good in her*, Esther thought. *Perhaps she's not as mean as she makes out. Still, I can't see how Jacob would want to be with someone who can be so mean at times.*

Esther felt guilty for thinking Jessie was mean. After all, there was only one Judge and it wasn't her place to judge others.

"Esther, why have your cheeks gone red?" Mary asked from across the room.

"I don't know," Esther said.

As Katie Hostetler walked over to Mrs. Miller, Esther held her breath. "How is Hannah doing, Rachel?"

"She is good, *denki*," Mrs. Miller said. Her tone was tense but not unkind. "I'm sure this will be a fine healthy *boppli*."

The two women smiled at each other and Esther breathed a sigh of relief. It really did seem that this baby had brought them together. Maybe her mother would stop trying to force her to marry Amos and allow her to marry Jacob.

Esther caught herself again. Whatever was she thinking? Her courtship, her fake courtship with Jacob was just that—a fake courtship. If only it had been real, as it seemed her mother would now permit a relationship between the two of them. But what point was there? Jacob was now courting Jessie. Maybe he liked girls with a little more spirit or a little bit of wickedness to them.

Jessie still reeked of cigarette smoke. It was surely obvious to everyone and Esther wondered why Beth Yoder hadn't said something to Jessie about it. Or maybe she had. Esther silently chided herself for judging again.

The headache was getting worse, so Esther said to Mrs. Yoder, "I have the beginnings of a headache. May I have some peppermint oil, please?"

"Yes, of course, you poor girl. I'll fetch some at once," Beth said, but Jessie jumped up.

"I'll take Esther to get it," Jessie said.

Esther caught her breath. Whatever was Jessie up to now?

Jessie took Esther by the arm and guided her into the kitchen. She reached up into a tall, green cupboard and pulled down a small amber bottle. "I made this myself," she said. "I use a lot of peppermint oil."

"Yes, I often smell it on you," Esther said without thinking.

Jessie looked surprised and then narrowed her eyes. "Here you are."

Esther thanked her. She dabbed some on her temples and then handed the little bottle back to Jessie.

"Jacob wrote some beautiful words on the card to me," she said. "I had no idea he was such a romantic *mann*."

"But I thought that card was from the whole Hostetler *familye*," Esther said, confused. Surely Mrs. Hostetler would know if Jacob had written something personal on the card.

Jessie laughed. "*Nee*, I'm not talking about the card Mrs. Hostetler gave me. Jacob was over earlier and gave me a personal card. He had written such beautiful words on it."

"That's nice," Esther said in the most even tone she could muster.

Jessie patted her shoulder, much like someone would pat a pet's head. "I don't mean to be rubbing it in, Esther. I know you liked him even though you're only pretending to date him. I hope I haven't upset you or hurt your feelings."

"No, not at all," Esther said. "I'm happy for you both." She sent up a silent prayer to *Gott* to forgive her for lying.

"*Denki* for keeping my secret," Jessie said. "Soon everyone will know about us, though."

"Everyone will know?" Esther parroted. She wondered why everyone would soon know.

"There is going to be a big announcement," Jessie pronounced smugly.

Chapter Twenty-One

When Esther opened the door a little way, she heard crying. She pushed the door fully open and hurried in. Mary was sitting on the couch, sobbing, and Mrs. Miller was sitting next to her, awkwardly patting her hand.

"What has happened?" Esther asked urgently.

"It's my mother," Mary said. "She's had an accident."

All sorts of horrible thoughts raced through Esther's head. "Is she all right?" she asked in a small voice.

Mrs. Miller stood up. "Mary's *mudder* was on a ladder cleaning the gutters and she fell. She is in the hospital. Mary's brother, John, called your *vadder*."

"Is John coming to collect Mary so she can visit her *mudder*?" Esther asked.

Mrs. Miller shook her head. "*Nee*, John accompanied his mother to the hospital as his father is sick with the flu. That's why Mary's mother was cleaning the gutters in the first place."

Esther was taking it all in when Mrs. Miller spoke

again. "Esther, your father and I have decided that you will take Mary to see her mother."

"Sure. Of course," Esther said. "I'd be happy to."

"Really?" was all Mary said. She dabbed her eyes with a tissue once more.

Esther was alarmed to see Mary's eyes red and puffy. "Do you know what your mother's injuries are?"

Mary shook her head and burst into a fresh round of tears.

"Esther, don't ask such questions," Mrs. Miller scolded her. "How can you be so senseless? Now, don't worry about me. Martha and Rebecca are getting better by the day and they can help me here. If I need any extra help I can always call on Hannah." She thought some more. "Actually, I won't call on Hannah since she is having a baby, but I won't need any help anyway. Now you two girls hurry and get ready and then Mr. Miller will call a driver to take you to your mother, Mary."

"*Denki, denki.*" Mary ran over and hugged Mrs. Miller, who stood there shocked, her hands by her sides. Finally she reached up and awkwardly patted Mary twice on the back.

Outward displays of affection were not common among the Amish, at least not in Esther's community. Esther allowed herself a small smile despite the enormity of the situation.

It didn't take Esther long to get ready. "Say goodbye to Hannah for me," she said to her *mudder*.

"We'll miss you," Martha said.

"But it's good that you're helping Mary," Rebecca added.

"Take as long as you like, Esther," Mrs. Miller said. She pressed some notes into Esther's hand. "Put this money in your purse."

Esther's eyes widened when she saw the amount of money, but she figured she would have to pay the driver there and the driver back, and she would need money while she was staying with Mary's parents.

Mrs. Miller addressed Mary. "Now Mary, we would like you back here, but if you need to stay with your mother, don't feel obliged to return."

"*Denki*," Mary said through her tears.

Mr. Miller had called for a driver, and she didn't take long to arrive. Her name was Charlotte. She was an *Englisch* lady, and she had driven Esther on previous occasions from time to time.

Charlotte was a pleasant woman. Esther liked to look at her makeup and earrings. She wore large silver earrings with intricate patterns on them, and bright, garish candy-pink lipstick. Her eye shadow was bright blue and Esther always wondered about her eyelashes. Surely they couldn't be real? Charlotte's eyelashes were as long as a horse's, but much thicker. Esther wondered if they were false and if so, how Charlotte managed to attach them to her eyes without doing herself an injury.

Charlotte tried to make conversation. "I haven't driven you out of your community before, Esther."

"My friend Mary here lives in another community and her mother's had an accident."

Charlotte was genuinely concerned. "Oh my gosh, that's terrible. Is she all right?"

Esther shot a look at Mary, fearful that Charlotte's words would set Mary off into a fresh bout of crying. "We don't quite know yet," Esther said.

"How did it happen?" Charlotte said. "Was it a buggy accident?"

"No, Mary's mother was up a ladder, cleaning gutters."

Charlotte made a clicking sound with her tongue. "Well, I hope everything is all right. How long are you staying there, Esther?"

"I don't know, but I'll call for you to drive me home, if that's all right."

"Sure it is, Esther," Charlotte said. "And I wish you all the luck in the world. Oh, I forgot. You Amish don't believe in luck, do you?"

"Not exactly," Esther said. She didn't want to explain the Amish ways at this time because she was concerned about Mary. Mary normally chatted nonstop, but right now she was silent and it unnerved Esther.

Luckily, Charlotte soon changed the subject. "That's a lot of rain we had the other day. It was well needed, wasn't it?" she said. Without waiting for a response, she pushed on. "My roses certainly needed it, although it's not always good to have rain and heat on roses at the same time. It causes black spot. I've had trouble with aphids lately. Have you had trouble with aphids, Esther?"

"On the roses?" Esther said absently.

"Yes, on the roses," Charlotte said.

"No, I boil garlic in water and then strain it and spray it on the roses. It keeps the aphids away," Esther said.

Charlotte made an appreciative grunt. "I'll have to try that. I've been spraying them with a pesticide, but it doesn't seem to help."

"That would also kill the natural predators of the aphids," Esther said, "but the garlic spray doesn't. Oh, I forgot. I also put some soap flakes into the mixture and dissolve them with the garlic. It seems to stop the aphids clinging to the roses."

"Another good tip, thank you," Charlotte said.

Charlotte continued to make small talk with Esther about the garden and the weather, but Mary remained silent the whole time, much to Esther's concern.

Two hours later, they arrived at the hospital. "I'll leave you here," Charlotte said. "Best of luck, or whatever it is that you believe in, Esther and Mary."

Esther thanked Charlotte and paid her. Charlotte gave a little wave and then drove away. Esther took Mary by the arm. "Where do we go?" Mary said in a small voice.

"I have no idea, to be honest," Esther said. "Let's go and find some signs."

They walked into the building, which was large and modern, clearly having been built in recent years. It didn't have any of the pungent antiseptic smell that some hospitals have. Esther had had enough of hospitals and would be happy never to set foot in one again. She knew they did good and healed people, but she had spent too much time in one of late and Rebecca had only just returned home from a lengthy stay in the hospital.

"Do you know what room your mother is in?" Esther asked Mary.

Mary looked stricken. "No, I don't have a clue. What if we can't find her?" All the color drained from Mary's face, and Esther feared she would faint.

"Don't worry, Mary," she said. "We can find her. We only need her name."

Mary took a deep gulp of air. "Are you sure?"

"Yes, of course I'm sure. Do you want to come with me or would you rather sit there until I come back for you?" Esther nodded to rows of chairs, most of which were filled with people.

Mary clutched her arm. "I'll come with you," she said. Mary and Esther wandered through the labyrinthine hospital corridors until they found a nurses' station.

Esther walked straight over to a nurse. "My friend, Mary Beiler here has been summoned to the hospital because her mother, Naomi Beiler, was in an accident today. It was a few hours ago," Esther said. "We've driven a long way to get here and we don't know where she is."

The nurse gave her a warm smile. "There's no need to be worried. What did you say her name was again?"

"Naomi Beiler," Mary said. "She's my mother. She was cleaning a gutter and she fell off the ladder."

Mary's eyes crinkled and she blew her nose violently, startling the nurse.

The nurse tapped away at the keyboard and peered at her computer. "Yes, she was in emergency and she's just now been moved to a room."

"Is she all right?" Mary asked urgently.

"She's in a normal room not in intensive care or anything," the nurse said, "but as for anything else, you'll have to ask her doctor."

"What room is it?" Mary asked.

"Room 505," the nurse said. She gave directions, which Esther tried to remember.

"Why couldn't she tell me if my mother's all right?" Mary asked Esther as they headed for the elevators.

"She must be fine or she would be in intensive care or something," Esther said. "That's a really good sign, Mary."

They walked into the elevators and Esther pressed the button to shut the door. As they were half way closed, a woman jumped in. Her floral perfume was overpowering and Esther sneezed repeatedly. When the woman got out a floor earlier, Esther noticed that Mary was crying, quietly this time.

"Don't worry, Mary," Esther said. "You'll be seeing your mother very soon." They walked out of the elevators, down a long corridor and then turned left. They continued down there until they found a nurses' station. A male nurse was standing there looking at a clipboard.

"Hi, I'm Mary Beiler and my mother, Naomi

Beiler, has been in an accident," Mary said. "The nurse downstairs told us we would find her in Room 505."

"Yes, feel free to go along," the man said, pointing over his shoulder.

Esther could see Mary wanted to ask the man more, but she could equally see the man was engrossed in what he was doing, so she gave a little tug on Mary's arm. "Your mother is just down there," she said. "Come on."

Mary hurried past her and strode down the corridor. By the time Esther reached the door she could hear voices. She knocked and walked in. The woman in the hospital bed looked a lot like Mary, with dark eyes and dark hair. Her arm was in plaster, but she was sitting up. Esther was relieved to see that Mary's mother didn't look too bad after all.

"What's wrong with you, *Mamm*?" Mary asked.

"Don't cry, Mary," her mother said. "I'm fine. And you must be Esther, Mary's friend."

Esther shyly walked around the bed. "Mary's been very worried about you."

Mary's mother looked stricken. "I'm so sorry you were worried about me, Mary. I've had X-rays. My arm's broken, but it's set now. The doctor said it's a good break." She laughed. "Imagine that—a good break. How can a break be good? And I also hit my head on the way down." She touched her head and then said, "Ouch. That's why I have to stay in overnight, just in case I have a concussion."

"Do the doctors think you have a concussion?" Mary asked, her voice filled with alarm.

"*Nee*, child, *nee*," her mother said. "They don't think I do. It's just procedure to keep someone who's had a bump on the head in overnight. I think my arm took my full weight."

"That's terrible, *Mamm*," Mary said. She took a deep breath and then burst into a fresh round of tears. Her mother reached out and patted her with her good arm. Esther hurried over and patted her on her back. To Mary's mother, Esther said, "I think these are tears of relief, because Mary was so worried about you all the way here."

"It was so good of you to bring Mary. I can't thank you enough," Mary's mother said. "Please call me Naomi."

Esther shot her a small smile.

Just then, John walked in carrying two steaming polystyrene cups of coffee. "*Hiya,* Mary, it's so good to see you. *Hiya*, Esther. You two must be tired."

Mary ran over to hug her brother, who held both cups out to the side so they wouldn't spill. Esther wondered if people in Mary's community were used to such outward displays of affection in public. When Mary finally released him, John said, "I'm sorry, I didn't know you were here already. I'll go back and fetch you some *kaffi*. You could use some after your long journey."

"Sure could," Mary said. "I'm so pleased to see you, John. I've missed you. I've had a good time at the Millers, mind you, but I've missed you too."

"Our mother is in dire need of *kaffi,"* John said with a chuckle. He hurried over and set the coffee on the little table next to his mother. "Esther and Mary, one of you can have my *kaffi* and I'll go and get two more," he said. He handed the cup to Mary and hurried out the door.

"You can have my *kaffi*, Esther," Mary said.

Esther held up one hand, palm outward, in protest. "I wouldn't hear of it. You have it, Mary. I insist."

Mary would have protested again but Esther put on her sternest expression and crossed her arms over her chest. Mary's face broke out into the first smile Esther had seen in a few hours.

"*Denki*, Esther," Mary said as she sipped the coffee. It certainly seemed to do the trick because her features relaxed at once.

Soon John returned with two more cups of coffee. He handed one to Esther. "How are things, Esther?" he said. "Mary writes me long letters, but they're all about her dog called Pirate."

Esther chuckled. "Mary sure is attached to that dog. We drive over there all the time so she can play with him."

"A neighbor's house burned down the other day," Mary said. "No one was hurt, but one of them is staying with the Millers. She's actually staying in the *grossmammi haus* with me."

"That's nice," Naomi said, but she stopped speaking when she caught Mary's expression.

"I heard your husband has had the flu quite badly," Esther said to Naomi.

It was John who answered. "Yes, he got a really nasty dose of the flu and he's cross with *Mamm* for climbing up on the roof. He wanted to take her to the hospital, but the doctor insisted that he stay home and rest."

Naomi laughed. "Poor Henry. He must be really upset that he can't see me. He's only just getting over the flu now. I've been waiting for weeks for him to clean out those gutters, so I thought I might as well do it myself. It had been raining and my feet just gave way. I must have slipped. I had nothing to grab onto and so I fell right on my poor arm."

"Does it hurt?" Mary said.

Her mother shook her head. "*Nee*, not at all, not if I don't move it. It hurt when they were setting it, but it doesn't hurt now. It's such a nuisance. I don't know how I'm going to get anything done with it."

"I'll stay and help you," Mary said.

"We'll see," Naomi said. "Esther, you're welcome to stay with us as long as you like. It is not a bad break, only a hairline fracture, and the doctor said I will soon have use of it again. I know Mary enjoys staying with your *familye*. Do you know if your mother would like to have her back?"

"Yes, *Mamm* would like Mary to come back, but only if it doesn't inconvenience you," Esther said.

"Would you mind staying for the next week or so and see how my arm comes along?" Naomi said. "If it looks like I can cope with my arm after a week or two, then you and Mary can return together."

"Yes, that would be good." Esther's heart was still

breaking over Jacob, and she was glad of the distraction. In fact, this was the first time she had thought about Jacob since they had entered the hospital. The long car ride though, had been another matter. She had thought about Jacob the whole time.

Still, the visit with the Beiler *familye* would certainly help her take her mind off him, and there would be no Jessie Yoder popping up from time to time to gloat about her relationship with Jacob.

Chapter Twenty-Two

John drove Mary and Esther to the Beilers' house. A man was sitting on the front porch on an old Adirondack chair. Esther figured he was Mr. Beiler. John pulled the horse to a stop and hopped down from the buggy. "This is my *vadder*, Henry Beiler," he said. "*Datt*, this is Esther Miller."

"*Hullo* there, Esther," Henry said. "Please call me Henry. Mary, it's so *gut* to see you! How is Naomi?" He addressed the latter to John.

"*Mamm* has a small fracture in her arm and they are only keeping her in overnight to see if she has a concussion. It's just routine. The doctor told me she would likely be released tomorrow morning."

Henry breathed a long sigh of relief. "I was so anxious when your mother fell from the ladder. Mary, get a bed ready for your friend."

"Sarah is going to help until *Mamm* gets back," John said. He beamed, and Esther thought perhaps John now had a girlfriend.

Mary hurried back down the stairs. “Sarah!” she shrieked. “I’m so pleased, John.” Before John could respond, Mary bounced back up the stairs.

Esther looked at John to see his face was beet red.

“That must be her now,” John said when there was a knock at the door. He crossed to the door and presently ushered in a short, pleasant girl whom he introduced as Sarah.

“How is Mrs. Beiler?” Sarah asked.

John filled her in as Mary popped down the stairs and beckoned to Esther. “Come on, Esther. I’ll show you to your room.”

Esther hurried up the stairs. The room had a lovely view of the rolling fields outside. Esther threw herself down on the bed. The sheets smelled strongly of lavender and Esther wondered if they had been left out to dry on the lavender bushes. “I’m so tired I could sleep for a week.”

Mary laughed. Esther was pleased to see Mary looking so happy after the shock of her mother’s accident.

“Maybe you should have a little nap.”

Esther sat up and rubbed her eyes. “*Nee*, that would be rude, but I will have an early night if that’s all right.”

“Of course. I’m so glad you could see my home, Esther.”

“Me too,” Esther said, “and I’m so happy your *mudder’s* all right.”

Mary smiled.

Sarah proved a great help, and the three women

soon had dinner ready for John and Henry Beiler. Henry thanked them profusely. "How did Naomi seem?" he asked for the umpteenth time.

Mary and John exchanged glances. "*Mamm* is fine, *Datt*," John said.

"I'm just worried about her, is all," Henry said. "I was the one who should have been up on the roof." He put his head in his hands.

"*Mamm* will be home tomorrow," Mary said.

Esther was so tired she could barely stay awake. She felt her head getting ever closer to the table and then shook herself awake.

"Esther, you should go to sleep now."

"No Mary, I must help with the dishes after dinner," Esther said.

"I must insist you rest," Henry said. "You've been good enough to come here with my *dochder* and I would feel bad if you helped any more tonight. Sarah and Mary can help."

Both girls smiled widely at Esther so she decided to take up the offer. "*Denki*," she said. "If you'll excuse me, I'll go to my room."

Never had Esther seen a bed so inviting. She threw herself on the bed, fully dressed.

Esther awoke the next morning. She had not drawn the blinds, so the sun shone in. Esther jumped to her feet, realizing she had slept past sunrise. "They will think me so rude," she muttered to herself.

Esther was relieved that she felt more refreshed this morning. She didn't know why she had been so tired the night before, but she figured it was all the stress of Jacob. Maybe Lizzie and her mother were right, after all. Maybe Esther should marry Amos. After all, he was a good *mann*. There was nothing wrong with him. Jacob had taken away her one chance at happiness and she knew she wouldn't find love like that again. She would just have to make it work with someone else. And since her mother was so keen for her to marry Amos, why not him? Esther felt all the happiness had drained from her.

By the time Esther reached the kitchen, Mary had made *kaffi* for everyone.

"I'm so sorry I slept in," Esther apologized, but Mary waved her concerns away.

"You were so tired, Esther," she said. "I thought you would fall asleep at the dinner table."

"What time is your mother coming home today?" Esther asked her.

Mary shrugged one shoulder. "I don't know. John said she can come home as soon as the doctor signs her papers, but he doesn't know what time the doctor will see her."

Esther nodded slowly. "So it could be any time really."

Mary nodded. "*Jah*. John is going to call the hospital every hour from the barn and then go and fetch *Mamm*."

"How is your father feeling this morning?" Esther asked.

"*Datt* said he's really worried about *Mamm*," Mary said with a frown on her face.

Henry Beiler appeared at the kitchen door. He was clearly overwhelmed with worry about his *fraa*. "I hope Naomi doesn't have a concussion," he said for what seemed to Esther to be the millionth time. "I'm sure she doesn't, but I can't help worrying. I miss her too."

It was clear to Esther that Henry and Naomi were very much in love. *Maybe I should wait to find love after all,* she thought. She had all but resigned herself to marry Amos, but now that she saw the love between Mary's parents, her heart yearned for that romantic love once more. Henry and Martha Beiler had clearly been married for years and had grown-up children, John and Mary, yet the love between them was strong.

Esther made up her mind then and there. She would not marry Amos and she would wait until she had a *mann* who made her heart sing. Surely Jacob would see Jessie's true colors. It seemed a strange match to Esther. She just had to cling to hope.

Later, Esther and Mary were sitting on the porch, sipping lemonade. "I was thinking that I'd have to stay here for some time, but Sarah seems to have things well under control," Mary said. "I think if I go with you sooner than I planned, then Sarah can stay around longer."

It took Esther a while to realize what Mary meant. "Oh," she said, "you're thinking that with you away, Sarah will have a chance to come over and spend time with John."

Mary giggled. "That's exactly what I'm thinking. Still, we will probably have to stay here another week or two, if that's all right with you, Esther?"

Esther nodded. "Yes, I'm happy to stay as long as you like," she said. Esther had no wish to go back and face Jacob and Jessie, not yet. She needed to harden her heart first.

Jacob was distraught when he heard Esther had gone to Mary's community. How long would she stay there? Esther had left, upset over words from Jessie. Jacob had hoped to explain, but now Esther had gone and he didn't know how long she would be away. It tore at his heart.

What was he to do? He considered writing her a letter, but what would he say? He could scarcely pour out his heartfelt feelings in a letter, but if he didn't write to Esther, she would continue under the misapprehension longer.

He thought about it some more. Maybe he should write a letter and tell Esther he was missing her. Still, she might simply think he was continuing the pretext of their pretend dating.

Maybe he could hire a driver and visit Esther, but he had to stay and help on the farm, given the fact that he and his brothers were spending so much time helping lay the foundations at the Troyers' after the fire. No, he didn't have time to leave, not right now.

His only hope was that Esther would come back, and soon.

Esther was helping Mary in the vegetable garden when John came over to speak with them. "*Mamm* has been discharged and can come home! Let's go and fetch her."

A deep voice sounded behind her. "I'm going too."

"*Nee*, you can't," John told his father. "You've just had the flu."

"I'm feeling much stronger today," he said. Esther noticed he swayed ever so slightly. "You can drive the buggy, John, but I'm coming too."

John nodded.

Soon John was driving back in the direction of the hospital. This time, Esther was more able to take in the scenery. She had not been so far from home before. And while an *Englischer* would not consider Mary's home far from her own, it was a long way to an Amish person such as herself. The landscape was slightly different too, slightly drier, Esther fancied. The fields at her home were lush and green, and while these fields were green, there was just a hint of dryness to them.

"It's Room 505," John told his father as everyone hopped down from the buggy and John tied the horse to the hitching rail.

As they walked through the front door of the hospital, Mary's mother hurried to greet them. "Henry, what are you doing here!" she exclaimed. "You should be home in bed."

Henry waved his wife's protestations aside. "I'm much better now. The shock of your accident must have jolted the flu out of me." He chuckled.

Naomi took his arm and leaned on him. "Look

at us. Soon John and Mary will be putting us in the *grossmammi haus*." She chuckled too.

Esther stood back awkwardly, not knowing what to do, but John took Naomi's arm and hurried her in the direction of the buggy. It seemed Mary's parents were keen to put the hospital behind them as soon as possible.

"I can't wait to wrap some comfrey leaves around my arm and take some comfrey tea," Naomi said to Mary.

"Old Mrs. Graber back home did the same thing for us after our buggy accident," Esther told her.

Naomi appeared interested. "*Wunderbar*! *Gott* has a variety of plants for His children to use."

"I'm taking us all for a meal," Henry said firmly. "It is to celebrate you coming home from the hospital, Naomi, and..."

Mary's mother interrupted him. "But I was only in there one night and there's nothing much wrong with me, really."

Henry smiled at her. "And to welcome Mary home and to welcome Esther to our *familye*."

"When you say it like that," Naomi said, "who could object? Does that sound good to you, Esther?"

"Yes, *denki*," Esther said. She felt happy with this *familye*. It was how she wanted to be twenty or thirty years into the future, with a loving husband and some *kinner*.

They hadn't driven far when John reined in the horse. "This is my parents' favorite restaurant," he said.

Esther looked over at the building. She only saw

Englischers outside, but when she walked inside she saw several Amish people. An Amish girl caught Esther's eye and smiled.

Esther at once felt right at home. When they were all seated, Henry said, "Now eat anything you like. Eat up, all of you." To his wife, he said, "You must be starving after the hospital food."

"It wasn't too bad, but yes, I'm looking forward to some proper food," she said. "Henry, do you think Sarah will help around the house?"

"I can help around the house and Esther can too," Mary said.

"Oh yes, I meant when you leave," Naomi said. "The doctors said I only have a hairline fracture of my arm and that it will heal quickly, but I'm not to use it too much. It needs time to heal. I expect I might have trouble lifting heavy pots, but if I had some help here and there to prepare meals in advance, that would be good."

"Sarah would be happy to help," John said, beaming from ear to ear.

Esther only wished her own mother were so accommodating of her choices, but then again, maybe her mother had been right.

"And so do you have a young *mann* back in your community?" Naomi asked Esther.

Esther did not know how to respond, but Mary answered for her. "Oh yes, she is dating Jacob Hostetler. His brother, Noah, is married to her sister, Hannah. Imagine that! And everyone teases them because there are two more Hostetler *bruders* and two more

Miller *schweschders*. Everyone says it would be funny if those two sets got married to each other as well." Mary broke off and laughed.

Esther remembered that Mary only chatted incessantly when she was nervous and clearly she wasn't nervous now.

"But I don't have anyone yet," Mary said, her face falling.

"You did mention a young man in your letters," her mother said.

"Oh, David. He's just a friend," Mary said enthusiastically. "I wrote you how I found the dog, but Mrs. Miller doesn't like pets so David Yoder said he'd take him. David's mother, Beth, is a good friend of Mrs. Miller's. Anyway, Pirate was really skinny when I found him and now David has him looking really good and he's trained him too."

Esther noticed Henry and Naomi exchange glances and she knew they were thinking what she was thinking, that maybe Mary had more than a little crush on David Yoder. Esther wondered how David felt about Mary. Did he only see her as a friend? They certainly got on very well. She and Jacob had that same easy relationship.

Jacob. There was that word again, the cause of all her misery.

The waitress appeared at the table, her pen hovering over a notepad. "Ready to order?" She shot them all a winning smile.

Esther hurriedly looked at the menu. The others had already decided what they were having. Esther figured that maybe that was because this was their favorite restaurant. Maybe they ordered the same thing all the time.

Henry Beiler and his son John apparently had the same taste because both ordered chicken, pepper jack cheese, lettuce, tomato, and red onions on sourdough bread. Naomi ordered grilled Swiss cheese and sauerkraut on rye bread. Mary ordered waffle fries with cheese and a grilled chicken wrap with grilled green peppers, grilled onion, tomato, and mayonnaise. There were too many delightful options on the menu. Esther decided to order a grilled chicken wrap with bacon.

Henry Beiler ordered sodas for everyone. "Naomi, I'll cut your food into little pieces so you can manage with your right hand. Mary, it is *wunderbar* to have you home, and it's wonderful to meet you, Esther," he said. "I feel better already. I'm also happy that Mary is a good help to your *mudder*."

"Mary has been a great help," Esther said enthusiastically. "I don't know how *Mamm* would have managed without her, and Hannah too. Hannah had to help *Mamm* when Hannah was on crutches. I don't how she did it. The doctor had ordered her to keep off her leg, but she had to keep using it because my two younger sisters, Martha and Rebecca, and I were all on mattresses on the floor. We couldn't get up the stairs with our injuries and Hannah and *Mamm* had to tend to our needs. Hannah got really good at managing and carrying things while on her crutches."

"Yes, her leg did improve a lot after I got there," Mary said, "and now Hannah is having a baby."

"A baby!" Naomi said. Her face lit up. "*Wunderbar*!" She clasped her hands in delight. "Is that the first grandchild for your *mudder*?"

Esther smiled and nodded.

"And I'm sure it won't be the last," Naomi said with a chuckle and a wink at Esther.

I can't see that I'll be having any kinner, Esther thought sadly, *unless I do marry someone just out of friendship and not love like* Mamm *wants me to. Still,* Mamm *and Lizzie did say I shouldn't marry Jacob, and he's courting Jessie after all.*

Her face fell.

Apparently Naomi was quite perceptive because she asked Esther, "Esther, is something wrong? Have I said something to upset you?"

Esther plastered a smile on her face. "*Nee*, not at all."

After lunch, the *menner* went to buy some tools. "My husband has recovered quickly," Naomi said. "Only the other day he was barely able to sit up in bed."

"It was probably worry over you that made him get better quickly," Mary said. "I have to go to the bathroom. Make sure no one drinks my soda, won't you, *Mamm*?"

Naomi nodded.

"Who would drink your soda?" Esther asked, puzzled, but Mary was already out of earshot.

Naomi laughed. "When John and Mary were

younger, John used to eat any food that was around. He would eat and drink any leftover food. Mary soon ate everything in sight just to stop John from getting it and that's why she blames him for her being so plump now." Naomi laughed and Esther laughed too.

"Esther, I don't mean to pry, but you looked quite upset before. I do hope it wasn't something I said?"

Esther shook her head. She thought upon the matter and then added, "I would like to ask your advice, if you don't mind? I know we've only just met but I don't have anyone to turn to."

Naomi leaned across the table. "Of course. Whatever is the matter?"

"I don't really know where to start." Esther scratched her head and thought she had better speak quickly before Mary returned to the table. "Well, it's like this. My mother and her friend Lizzie tell me that childbearing years pass by in a flash and I have to basically marry any suitable man if I want to have *kinner*. Otherwise, life will pass me by. They don't seem so concerned with love or romantic feelings."

Naomi frowned so hard that her brows knit in the middle. "And you, Esther, what do you say?"

"I don't want to marry someone I see only as a friend," she said. "I want to marry a man I'm in love with. I've seen how you and Mr. Beiler are and you've obviously been in love for years. Were you in love when you first met?"

"Not when we first met, but soon after," Naomi said. "It took me a while to realize I was in love with him, but I most certainly was in love with him well before we were married. I'm like you, Esther—I couldn't marry someone I wasn't in love with. To me, romantic feelings are very important, but I know it's not the same for everyone. Everyone makes their own choices."

Esther nodded slowly.

"Do you have a particular young *mann* in mind?" Naomi asked her.

Esther nodded slowly. "*Jah.* Jacob Hostetler and I have been friends since we were children, but my mother wants me to marry Amos Troyer. He is nice and all that, but I don't feel anything for him. Anyway, my mother can get very insistent with her matchmaking so I asked Jacob to pretend to be dating me."

Naomi's eyes widened. "Did he agree?"

Esther nodded. "Yes. He agreed at once. He's such a good friend, you see. Anyway, he suggested we go on a buggy ride to keep up appearances."

"He did?"

Esther pushed on. "*Jah.* We've been on a buggy ride and we had a lovely picnic. You know how Mary always mentions David Yoder?"

Naomi nodded.

"David has a sister called Jessie. She came and told me in secret that she and Jacob are dating. She said I wasn't to tell anyone, but as you're not from our community, I'm sure it's okay to tell you, but please don't tell anyone else."

"No, I won't," Naomi said. "And why did you believe this girl? Is she particularly known for her honesty, if you get my meaning?"

Esther scratched her prayer *kapp.* "I don't particularly know. Are you saying she might have been lying?"

"I don't know the girl at all, but from what you've said to me, it does seem to be a possibility," Naomi said. "Why would Jacob so readily agree to pretend to be dating you otherwise? If he was secretly dating someone else, it would clearly hurt that girl's feelings, and no matter how good friends you are, his girlfriend would come first if he is a decent young man. *Nee*, as an outsider, I do wonder. Perhaps you should ask Jacob."

"That didn't even occur to me," Esther said. Could there be hope, after all? Was it possible that Jessie could be lying? She certainly hoped so. After all, it was something Jessie would do.

A little glimmer of hope arose in Esther, and that time, she allowed it.

Jacob was so busy hammering the nail that he didn't know someone was behind him. He heard a sound and spun around. To his displeasure, it was Jessie Yoder.

"Hi," she said.

He put down the hammer and crossed his arms over his chest. "*Hiya*, Jessie." Surely Jessie wasn't here to make more trouble? After his talk with her, he was sure she would back off, but it seemed that was not the case. "What are you doing here, Jessie?"

Jessie smiled from ear to ear, a sight that discomfited Jacob. He had never seen Jessie smile before and his instincts told him she was up to something.

"I just wanted to apologize for all the trouble I've caused."

Jacob narrowed his eyes and looked at her more closely. She certainly didn't seem sorry for the trouble she had caused. In fact, she was still smiling widely. "*Denki*," Jacob said. He hoped she would now leave.

"I heard Esther is coming back today."

So that's what it's all about, Jacob thought. "*Jah*, she's coming back this evening." *And I'm going over to speak with her tomorrow morning*, Jacob silently added.

"She's been away a long time, hasn't she? Two weeks?"

Jacob nodded. "Was there something in particular you are after, Jessie?" he asked, hoping his words did not sound too harsh.

She did not appear to mind. "*Nee*. I just wanted to apologize once more. I hope you and Esther are happy together. I really mean it."

Jacob was surprised at the words that came out of Jessie's mouth. Was she genuine? If so, he felt bad for thinking such thoughts of her. "*Denki*," he said.

"My mother sent me over here to ask a favor of you."

"Oh, what is it?" Jacob asked.

"My father and David have been over at the Troyers' house site every day and they have to be there tomorrow, but my mother has a chicken coop arriving at the freight depot. She wants me to be there at a quarter to nine tomorrow morning. She asked me to ask if you could drive me there. It will take two people to lift it."

"Will it fit in the buggy?" Jacob asked.

"Oh yes, it's in lots of pieces," Jessie said. "My mother asked if you'd mind doing this one small favor since my brother and my father can't do it."

"Would ten or eleven do?" Jacob asked.

For some reason, Jessie looked alarmed. "*Nee*. It must be at that exact time. My father called them and they said the chicken coop would definitely be in by that time and my mother needs it back in a hurry so she can go to town afterward."

"Sure," Jacob said. "I can have you there at a quarter to nine."

"*Denki*," Jessie said meekly. She at once left, leaving Jacob staring after her.

Maybe Jessie had changed her mind after all. She had seemed accepting of his relationship with Esther.

Jacob's heart ached for Esther. Two weeks had been a long time. He had known he was deeply in love with Esther before, but now he knew he could not bear to spend a minute without her. He knew for a fact that *Gott* had chosen Esther for him, but worry lay heavily on his heart. What if Esther had fallen in love with someone in Mary's community?

Jacob wasn't usually a jealous person, but he could not help but be concerned. Esther had left under a cloud and he hoped that cloud hadn't pushed her into the arms of another man.

Chapter Twenty-Three

The next morning, Esther arrived in her buggy to collect Hannah from Mrs. Hostetler's store. They were headed to the outskirts of town to pick up a delivery of fabric supplies from the freight depot. The local carrier charged far too much to deliver directly to the quilt store. Hannah and Esther did this regularly, on one Wednesday morning a month, arriving at the depot at precisely nine.

Hannah and Esther were walking to Esther's buggy, and as they arrived there, Albrecht Graber pulled his horse in next to them and waved to them. "*Hiya*, Hannah and Esther."

"*Hiya*, Albrecht," they both said.

Albrecht walked over to them. "You work for Mrs. Hostetler, don't you, Hannah?"

Hannah nodded, and Esther said, "Yes, we're just on the way to the freight depot for her now. We're in a bit of a rush as we have to be there at nine." Esther knew that the kindly Albrecht would talk for hours if given the opportunity. He was just like Mary in that way.

Albrecht laughed. "She won't mind if you're late, just this one time, what with Jacob about to be married."

Esther heard Hannah gasp. "What? What did you say?" Esther stammered.

Albrecht flushed red. "Oh, I thought Mrs. Hostetler would've already told you. Me and my big mouth! Don't tell anyone, will you? I saw Jacob buying an engagement gift for Jessie Yoder. He wouldn't want me to say."

"Are you sure?" Hannah asked.

"Oh yes, of course he wouldn't want me to say. You know how these things are always kept secret." Albrecht's hand flew to his mouth. "Oh silly me. I mean yes, he was buying engagement gifts for Jessie Yoder. He bought her a clock and a teapot. I'd better be going. Please don't tell anyone, will you." Albrecht looked shame-faced, and departed in a hurry.

Esther felt numb. She climbed in the buggy and took up the reins.

Hannah turned to her. "*Nee*, Esther, Albrecht's mixed up! That can't be right."

Tears rolled down Esther's cheeks, and Hannah didn't speak again for a while. Soon they were driving along through rolling hills dotted with wildflowers of blue, white, and yellow. A truck went past, a little too fast and close for comfort, but this was not a busy road, and they met no other traffic.

Esther was heartbroken over the news that Jessie

was engaged to Jacob, *her* Jacob. She had cried herself to sleep the night before, and her eyes were sore. She thought things were bad last night, but now they were infinitely worse. How could this be? Jessie and Jacob, engaged?

Esther mulled over whether to tell Hannah but thought she had best not, given that Hannah was married to Jacob's *bruder*. Jessie had asked her not to tell anyone, after all, and Hannah was likely to tell her husband Noah, who no doubt would tell his *bruder*, Jacob. Silence was clearly the best policy here, she considered.

As they approached the freight depot, Esther could see a buggy approaching them in the distance. "Who could that be?" Hannah wondered aloud.

Esther squinted against the sun's rays. "We'll soon know."

As the two buggies drew closer to each other, Esther's mouth ran dry. It was Jacob's buggy, and there sitting next to him, was Jessie. Hannah said, "Stop, Esther," when Esther made no move to do so, but Esther pushed the horse on faster. Esther just had time to register the surprise on Jacob's face when she didn't stop, but trotted on. Jacob had been in the process of stopping his buggy.

Esther saw a wide smile from Jessie, but she simply waved to them rather stiffly and then looked straight ahead. If Esther harbored any doubt before, she did not now. The evidence was right there in front of her nose, and there was no escaping it any longer—Jacob and Jessie were clearly engaged. For one thing, no one else but Hannah knew of their planned pretense, and secondly, Jacob and Jessie were on a buggy ride together. Plus Albrecht Graber had seen Jacob buying engagement gifts for Jessie. Esther had tried to be in denial and not face facts, but that was no longer possible.

Hannah looked over at Esther. "What's going on, Esther? Why didn't you stop for Jacob?"

"I didn't want to disturb Jacob and Jessie."

"Why ever not?"

Esther just shrugged and hoped Hannah wouldn't pursue this line of questioning. Fortunately, they had arrived at the freight depot so Hannah was kept busy with Mrs. Hostetler's order.

When the fabric was safely loaded, the girls headed back to town. Yet no sooner than Esther had taken up the reins, than Hannah turned to her. "Now, tell me. What's going on? Why didn't you want to speak to Jacob?"

Esther sighed. "I can't really say."

"Why not? Look, Esther, what's this all about? You're being awfully mysterious."

Esther hadn't planned to tell Hannah, but the words just came tumbling out. "Oh, Hannah, I'm so upset. I wanted to tell you, but she made me promise not to tell anyone. And you can't keep a secret from Noah, so you'll tell Noah, and he can't keep a secret from his *bruder*, so he'll tell Jacob. And I don't want Jacob to know." With that, Esther burst into a flood of tears.

"Oh, Esther, please don't cry. Please tell me what's going on. I don't understand anything you just said."

Esther fought to control her tears, and blew her nose loudly into a tissue. "It was Jessie! She made me promise not to tell." Her voice came out between sobs.

"Jessie Yoder? I don't understand. You'd better start from the beginning."

Esther took a deep breath. "You know how I asked Jacob to pretend we were dating, so *Mamm* wouldn't push me onto Amos?"

Hannah nodded. "*Jah*, and how did that go?"

"It went okay, but Jacob was only doing it to help me out, but he's secretly been dating Jessie Yoder."

"*Nee*, that's not right."

"I was shocked too, Hannah," Esther said, "but it's true. You didn't tell anyone that Jacob and I were pretending to date, did you?"

"*Nee*, of course not."

"Well, Jessie came to our *haus* the other day. She said that Jacob told her that we were only pretending to be dating, and that he wanted to help me because I'm his oldest friend. Hannah, don't you see? It must be true, or how else would Jessie know that we were only pretending?"

Hannah was silent for a moment. "I don't know how she knew, but I'm sure that Jacob didn't tell her."

Esther allowed herself a small glimmer of hope before she pushed it away. "Jessie also said that she and Jacob have been secretly courting."

"*Nee, nee*," Hannah said. "I'm sure that's not right. Noah would know if they were."

"Hannah, she said *secretly*."

Hannah shook her head strongly. "*Nee*, Noah and Jacob are close. I'm sure this isn't right, Esther. Jessie has always had her heart set on Jacob, but he's always..." Hannah's voice trailed away, and then continued. "I truly don't believe what she said to you. It was just her way of trying to chase you away from Jacob. Now, I know what Albrecht Graber said, but I'm sure it's just a big misunderstanding. Maybe Jessie told him that."

Esther's heart soared. Could Hannah be right? Was this all a plot of Jessie's to drive a wedge between her and Jacob? Esther didn't want to get her hopes up, in case Hannah was wrong.

"Tell me this, Esther. Why were you so upset when you thought that Jessie and Jacob were dating? Have you finally realized how you feel about Jacob?"

Esther's hand flew to her throat. "What do you mean, Hannah? How did you know?"

Hannah laughed. "Everyone knew but you, Esther. I always knew you'd marry Jacob. You just had to come to terms with your feelings for him."

Esther sighed. "I think I've ruined everything, Hannah."

Hannah looked over at Esther and smiled. "You know what the ministers always say, 'Let go and let *Gott*.' When we think our paths are impossible, or at least horribly difficult, that's when *Gott's* light shines on our paths. *Gott* makes a way where there is no way. You'll see, Esther. If it's *Gott's* will for you and Jacob to be together, it will happen. But you can't carry this burden—give it to *Gott* and be still and accept His will."

Esther sighed. "I hope you're right."

Jacob's heart caught in his mouth when he saw Esther's buggy coming. *So this is why Jessie insisted I take her to the freight depot at precisely a quarter to nine in the morning, so Esther would see us,* he thought. *I knew something was wrong when the freight depot said that the chicken coop wasn't expected until next week.*

He looked over at Jessie and she was smiling, looking very pleased with herself. Jacob slowed his horse, fully intending to tell Esther that Jessie had asked him to drive her to the depot to lift the heavy framework for the Yoders' new chicken coop, but Esther did not stop the buggy.

Jacob was furious. Once again he had fallen foul of Jessie's plots. He clicked his horse on to go faster. Fifteen minutes later, they reached a Bed and Breakfast establishment on the outskirts of town. Jacob handed Jessie some money.

She looked up at him, puzzled. "What's this for, Jacob?"

"It's for you to go into that Bed and Breakfast and call a taxi to take you home. Jessie, I *am* going to the bishop about your behavior." He held up his hand as she made to speak. "Don't say a word! You'll make matters worse. I *am* going to marry Esther, and nothing you can do will stop that. I suggest you keep well out of my way in future. Get out of the buggy now."

Jessie's jaw dropped open. Jacob suspected that no one had ever spoken to her in such a way before. She glared at Jacob, but got out of the buggy. Jacob turned the buggy around and clicked up his horse in the direction of the Miller *haus*.

Chapter Twenty-Four

Esther drove under the shadows of the trees strung along the road. Unlike Jacob and Jessie Yoder, Esther had no partner to find comfort in, so she smoothed down her dress, held her head up, and tried to focus on her breathing on the long drive home, as tears welled up in her eyes.

Hannah had tried to convince her that things between Jacob and Jessie were not as they seemed. Esther had remained convinced while Hannah was still with her in the buggy, but once she had left Hannah back at the quilt store, Esther was no longer sure at all.

When Esther came around the last corner before arriving at her *haus*, her gaze fell upon a *mann* and his buggy silhouetted against the morning sun. As she approached, she saw that the *mann* was Jacob.

He was waving his arms urgently.

"Esther," he called, breathlessly. "Can we share a word? I really must insist."

Esther reined in her horse and got down from her

buggy. She walked over to Jacob, and stood before him, fidgeting under his handsome gaze. He had been waving to her frantically before she had stopped the buggy, and though Esther felt mighty silly for taking such a long time to recognize her feelings for Jacob, she desperately wanted to know what was going on.

Jacob held out his arm. "Come on a walk with me, won't you?"

Esther felt her heart pinch. She nodded, and followed Jacob to the creek.

The water was as clear as a summer's day, and it bubbled pleasantly as it weaved through the trees and the houses. Esther smoothed down her simple dress, watching as the sunlight through the trees dappled Jacob's golden skin. She had a million questions for him, but it was so nice to walk in silence for a time, especially after she had spent so much time in recent days thinking that Jacob was lost to her forever.

"I turned around as soon as I could," Jacob began. He reached up and plucked a leaf from the tree, rolling it through fingers hardened from years of farm work. "I don't think you understand, Esther."

"What do you mean?" she whispered, her throat dry.

She saw the muscles in his throat tighten as he shook his head. "I don't you think you understand at all."

Esther looked at the ground, hoping Jacob wouldn't notice that she was both bright pink and trembling.

"Let's get closer to the water," he added.

The earth was smooth, but occasionally she crossed the path of a stray rock or weed, and she did not want to take a tumble at this point in time.

"Jacob," she said now, "what don't I understand?"

"I am desperately and unashamedly in love with you."

Time seemed to freeze. Happiness was within her grasp, but one question remained unanswered. Esther's mind went back to this morning, when she saw Jessie Yoder in Jacob's buggy. Why was Jessie in his buggy, if they were not promised to each other? Why did Albrecht Graber think Jacob was buying engagement gifts for Jessie? What was going on?

"I don't understand," she said in a still, small voice.

"I know." Jacob's crooked smile lighted up his whole face. "I know. It is so confusing. Allow me to explain. This morning was not what you thought." He released the leaf and bent over to pull a duck weed from the bank of the creek, peeling off its fraying ends as they continued their walk. "Jessie and I are not together. She fooled me, and I should have noticed sooner."

"She fooled you into dating her?"

"*Nee*, Jessie and I were never together. She only wanted you to think that she and I were together. I'm afraid she's been spinning lies to you the entire time. I told her to stop interfering with us. She promised she would, and then she asked me to take her this morning to pick up a chicken coop. I didn't see then that she had ulterior motives."

"She had ulterior motives?" Esther parroted, trying to take in everything Jacob was saying. Could this be true? Could Jacob, *her* Jacob, truly be in love with her?

"Yes." Jacob's voice was grim now. "She wanted

you to see her in the buggy with me, to fool you into thinking she and I were together. It was devious and cruel of her."

So Jessie Yoder had been playing them all this whole time? Esther was relieved that Jacob was available, but she was also disappointed in Jessie Yoder. It was never kind to play with people's hearts like that. She sent a silent prayer of forgiveness toward Jessie and released that into *Gott's* hands.

Esther turned to face Jacob. "But this morning, Albrecht Graber said he saw you buying engagement gifts for Jessie Yoder."

Jacob shook his head. "*Jah*, Albrecht saw me buying gifts, but they weren't for Jessie Yoder. I suppose he assumed that Jessie and I were courting as he saw the fuss that Jessie made over me at the barn-raising, and he jumped to the wrong conclusions. He was sitting next to me then, you know."

Esther nodded. "I remember." The two started walking again.

"I'm so glad you and Jessie aren't together," said Esther, quietly.

Jacob stopped walking. "You are?"

"Oh, Jacob of course I am! You've been honest with me, so now I'll have to be honest with you. I am sorry I didn't realize it sooner, Jacob, but I'm in love with you too."

He dropped the weed and ran a hand through his hair, grinning down on Esther. "Are you sure?"

Esther smiled shyly up at him. "*Jah*, I am. I'm sorry it took me so long to know myself better."

Jacob and Esther now eased themselves onto the ground by the side of the creek, sunlight pressing into their bare faces and hands. It was gorgeous to sit here together, to know that everything was working out for the best.

Esther sighed with relief. Only minutes ago she was sitting by Hannah in the *familye* buggy, crying at the thought of losing Jacob. Now she sat by his side, blissfully happy. Jacob talked away, and the sound reminded Esther of the bubbling creek, cool and pleasant to listen to. It did not matter what he said. It just mattered that he said it, and that Esther was the one who was there to listen.

"Amos is in for a surprise," he was saying.

"My *mudder* too," replied Esther, quietly. She knew Amos wouldn't mind, and she already suspected he had eyes for her *schweschder*, Martha. A bird fluttered onto a nearby branch, hooting happily as the sun rose in the sky. "Noah and Hannah are in for a surprise too," Esther added, "although unlike my *mudder*, I'm sure they'll find this surprise a nice one."

Amos would no longer be held as a suitable husband for Esther; her *mudder* would no longer bother her, and she may now marry a man who was kind and compassionate and hard working.

She could not wait to tell Martha and Rebecca.

She knew they would tease her endlessly, but now Esther would have Jacob by her side, to laugh with her at their friendly teasing from now until forever.

* * * * *